P9-CFP-948

BOOK TWO IN THE DESCENDANTS SERIES

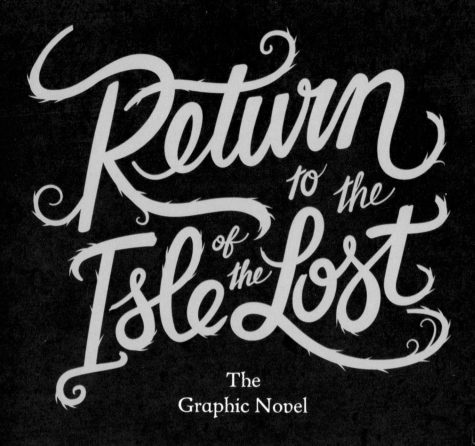

Return to the Isle of the Lost

The
Graphic Novel

#1 *New York Times* best-selling author
Melissa de la Cruz
Based on *Descendants*
written by Josann McGibbon & Sara Parriott

Adapted by
ROBERT VENDITTI

Art by
KRZYSZTOF CHALIK

Lettering by
CHRIS DICKEY

Adapted from the novel *Return to the Isle of the Lost*
Copyright © 2019 by Disney Enterprises, Inc.

All rights reserved. Published by Disney • Hyperion, an imprint of Disney Book Group. No part of this book may be reproduced or transmitted in any form or by any means, electronic or mechanical, including photocopying, recording, or by any information storage and retrieval system, without written permission from the publisher. For information address Disney • Hyperion, 125 West End Avenue, New York, New York 10023.

First Edition, July 2019
10 9 8 7 6 5 4 3 2 1
FAC-038091-19165
Printed in the United States of America

ISBN (hardcover) 978-1-368-04098-3
ISBN (paperback) 978-1-368-04187-4
Reinforced binding
Visit DisneyBooks.com
and DisneyDescendants.com

SUSTAINABLE FORESTRY INITIATIVE
Certified Sourcing
www.sfiprogram.org
SFI-00993
Logo Applies to Text Stock Only

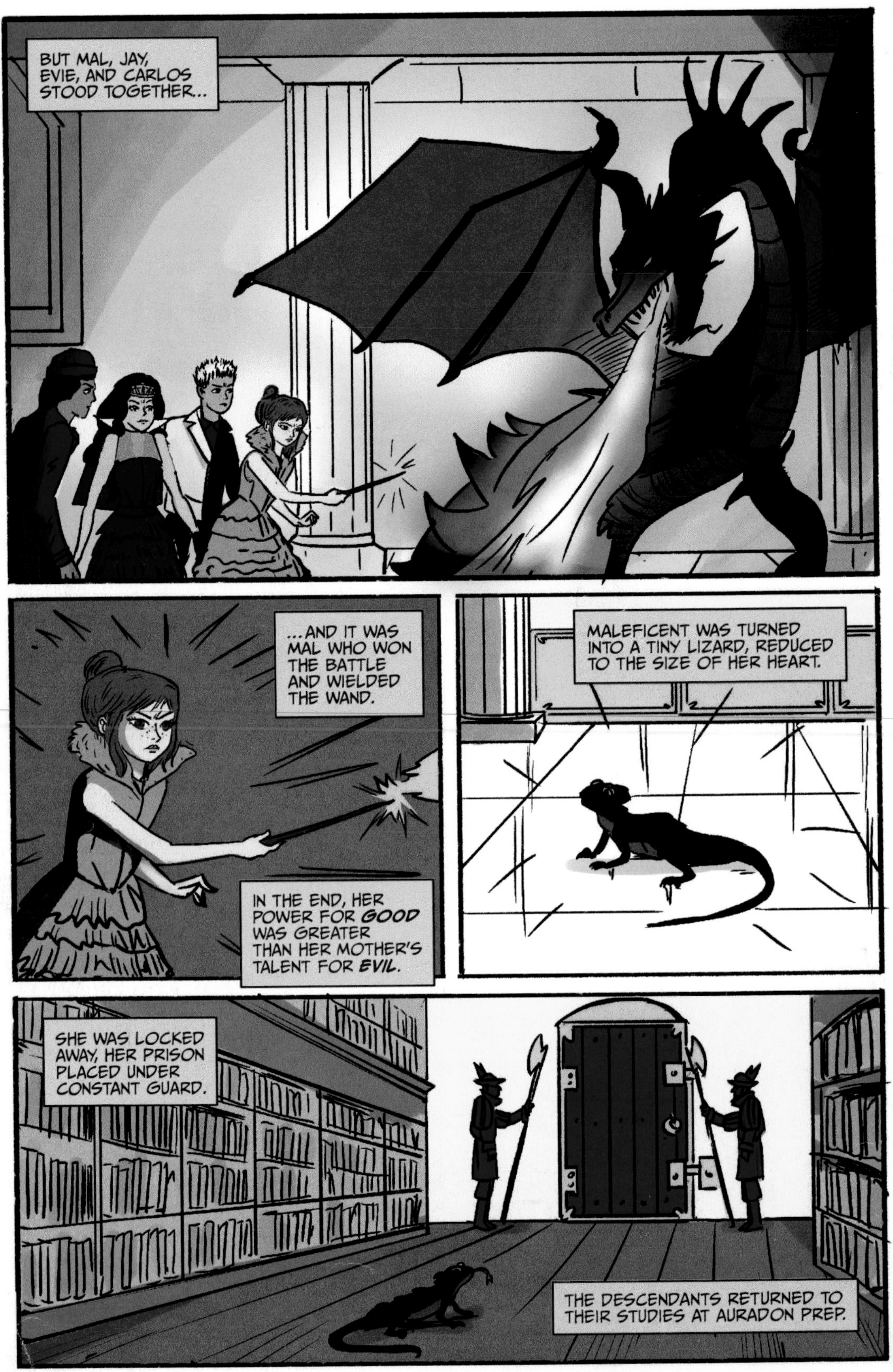
BUT MAL, JAY, EVIE, AND CARLOS STOOD TOGETHER...
...AND IT WAS MAL WHO WON THE BATTLE AND WIELDED THE WAND.
IN THE END, HER POWER FOR GOOD WAS GREATER THAN HER MOTHER'S TALENT FOR EVIL.
MALEFICENT WAS TURNED INTO A TINY LIZARD, REDUCED TO THE SIZE OF HER HEART.
SHE WAS LOCKED AWAY, HER PRISON PLACED UNDER CONSTANT GUARD.
THE DESCENDANTS RETURNED TO THEIR STUDIES AT AURADON PREP.

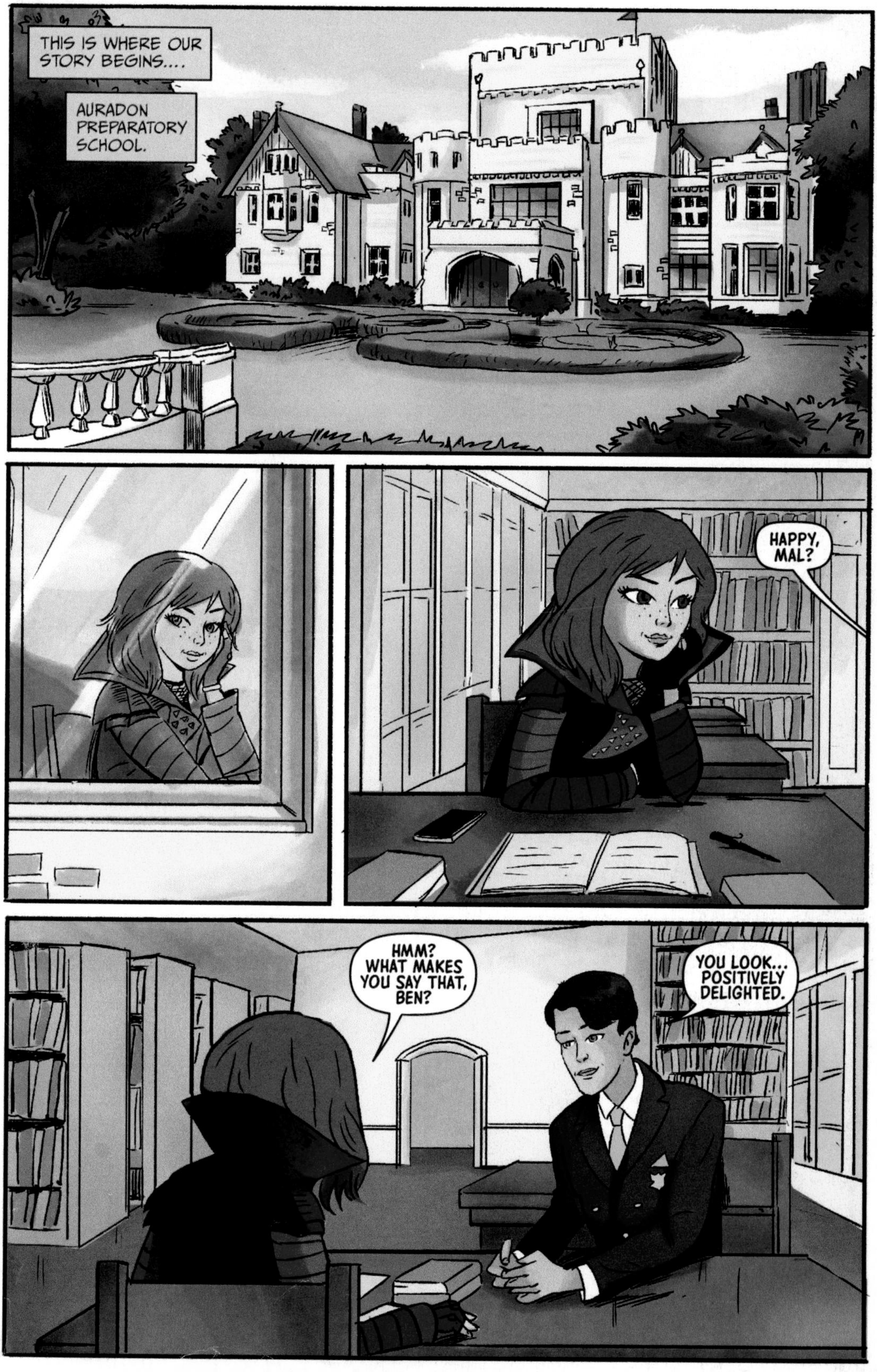
THIS IS WHERE OUR STORY BEGINS....
AURADON PREPARATORY SCHOOL.
HAPPY, MAL?
HMM? WHAT MAKES YOU SAY THAT, BEN?
YOU LOOK... POSITIVELY DELIGHTED.

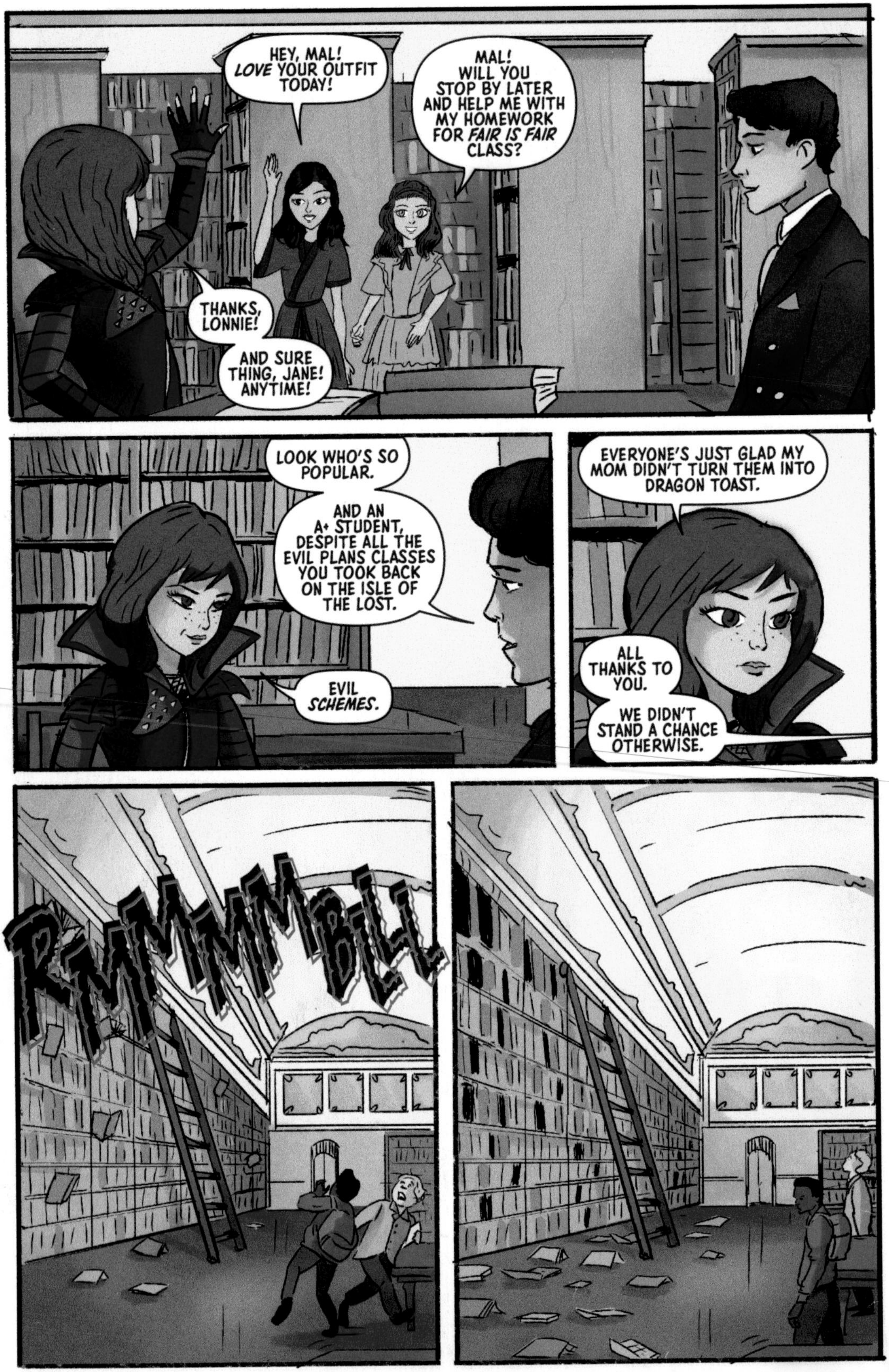
HEY, MAL! *LOVE* YOUR OUTFIT TODAY!
MAL! WILL YOU STOP BY LATER AND HELP ME WITH MY HOMEWORK FOR *FAIR IS FAIR* CLASS?
THANKS, LONNIE!
AND SURE THING, JANE! ANYTIME!
LOOK WHO'S SO POPULAR.
AND AN A+ STUDENT, DESPITE ALL THE EVIL PLANS CLASSES YOU TOOK BACK ON THE ISLE OF THE LOST.
EVIL *SCHEMES*.
EVERYONE'S JUST GLAD MY MOM DIDN'T TURN THEM INTO DRAGON TOAST.
ALL THANKS TO YOU.
WE DIDN'T STAND A CHANCE OTHERWISE.
RMMMMBLL

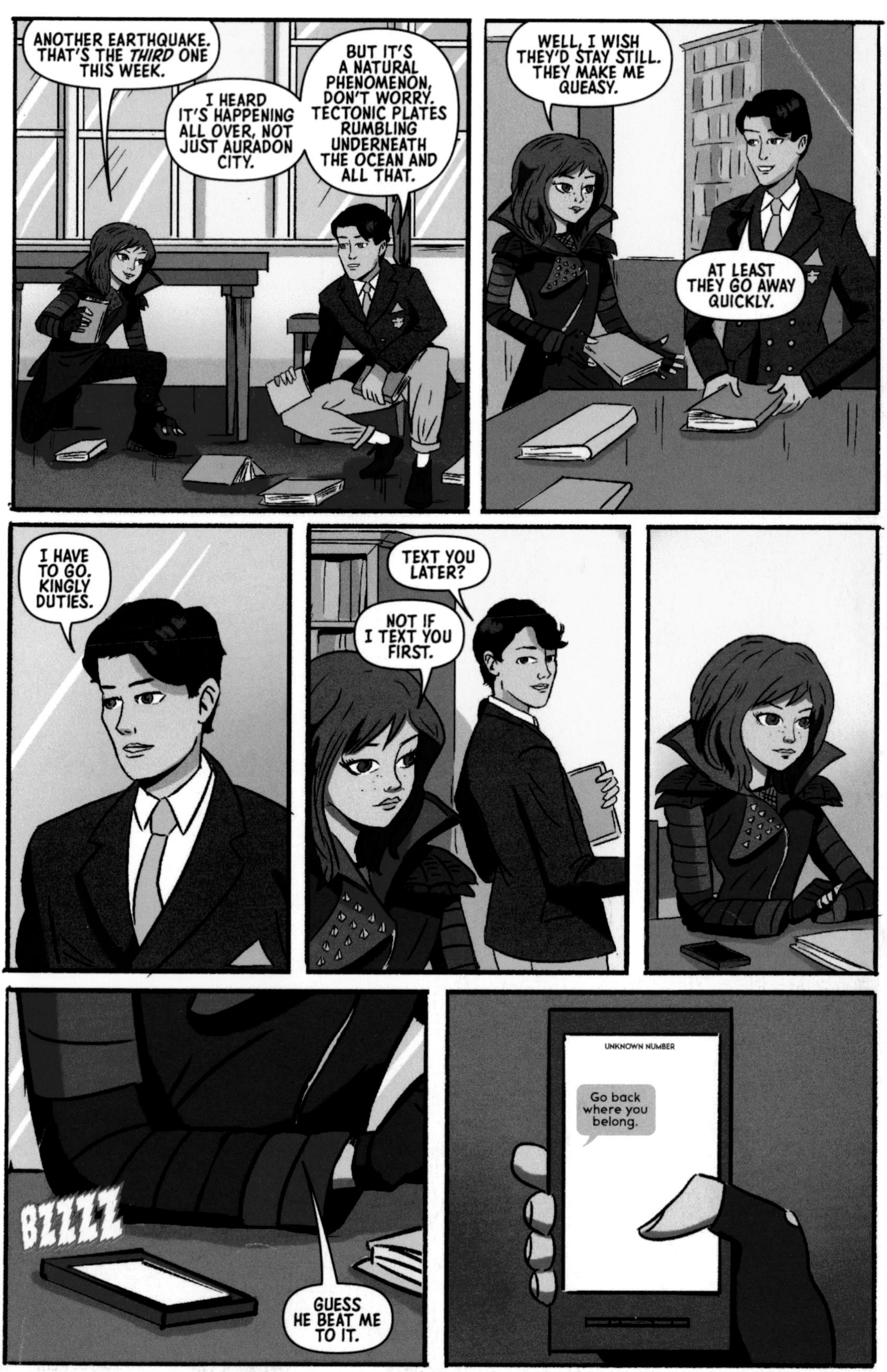
ANOTHER EARTHQUAKE. THAT'S THE *THIRD* ONE THIS WEEK.
I HEARD IT'S HAPPENING ALL OVER, NOT JUST AURADON CITY.
BUT IT'S A NATURAL PHENOMENON, DON'T WORRY. TECTONIC PLATES RUMBLING UNDERNEATH THE OCEAN AND ALL THAT.
WELL, I WISH THEY'D STAY STILL. THEY MAKE ME QUEASY.
AT LEAST THEY GO AWAY QUICKLY.
I HAVE TO GO. KINGLY DUTIES.
TEXT YOU LATER?
NOT IF I TEXT YOU FIRST.
BZZZZ
GUESS HE BEAT ME TO IT.
UNKNOWN NUMBER
Go back where you belong.

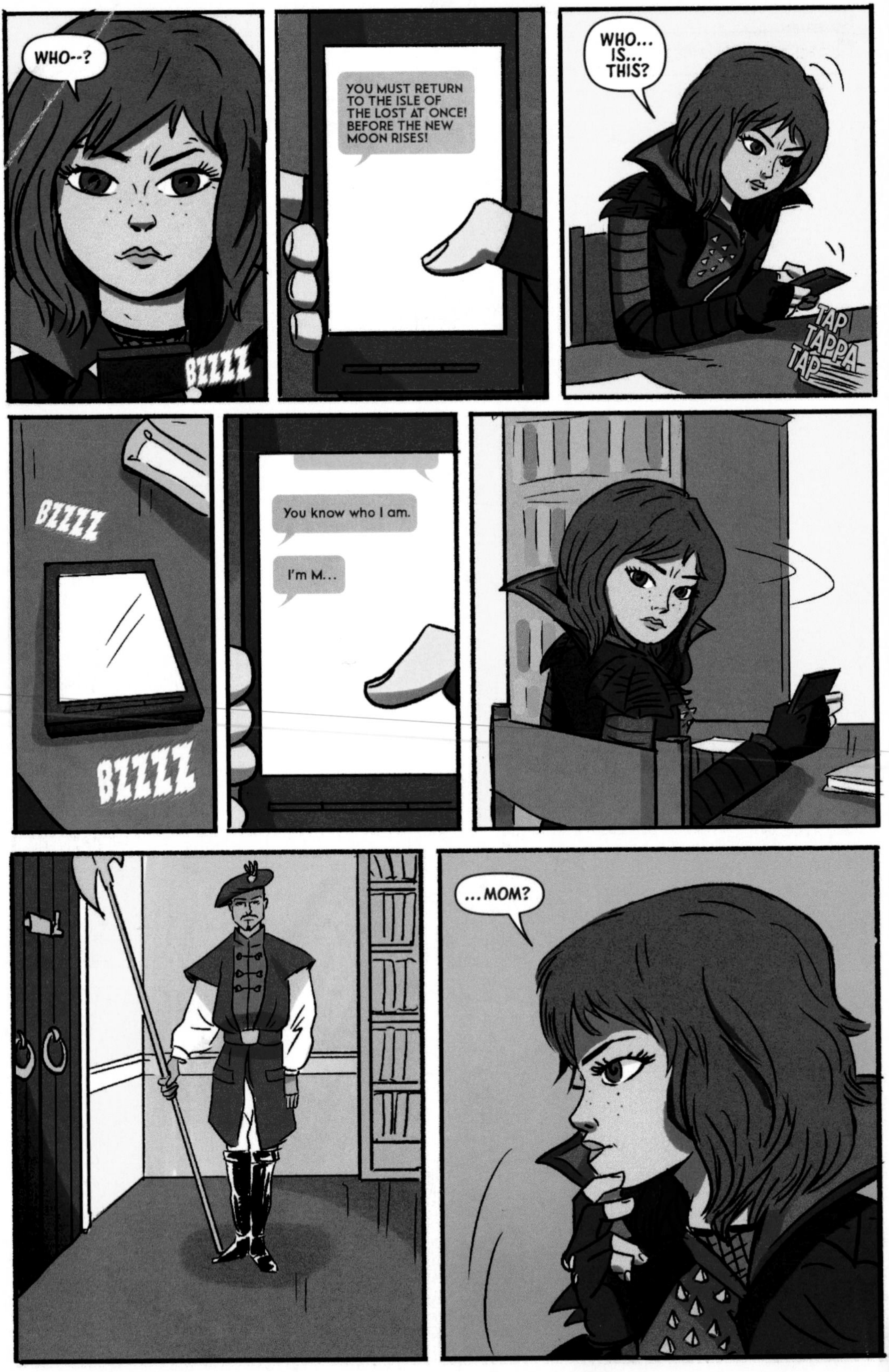
WHO--?
BZZZZ
YOU MUST RETURN TO THE ISLE OF THE LOST AT ONCE! BEFORE THE NEW MOON RISES!
WHO... IS... THIS?
TAP TAPPA TAP
BZZZZ
BZZZZ
You know who I am.
I'm M...
...MOM?

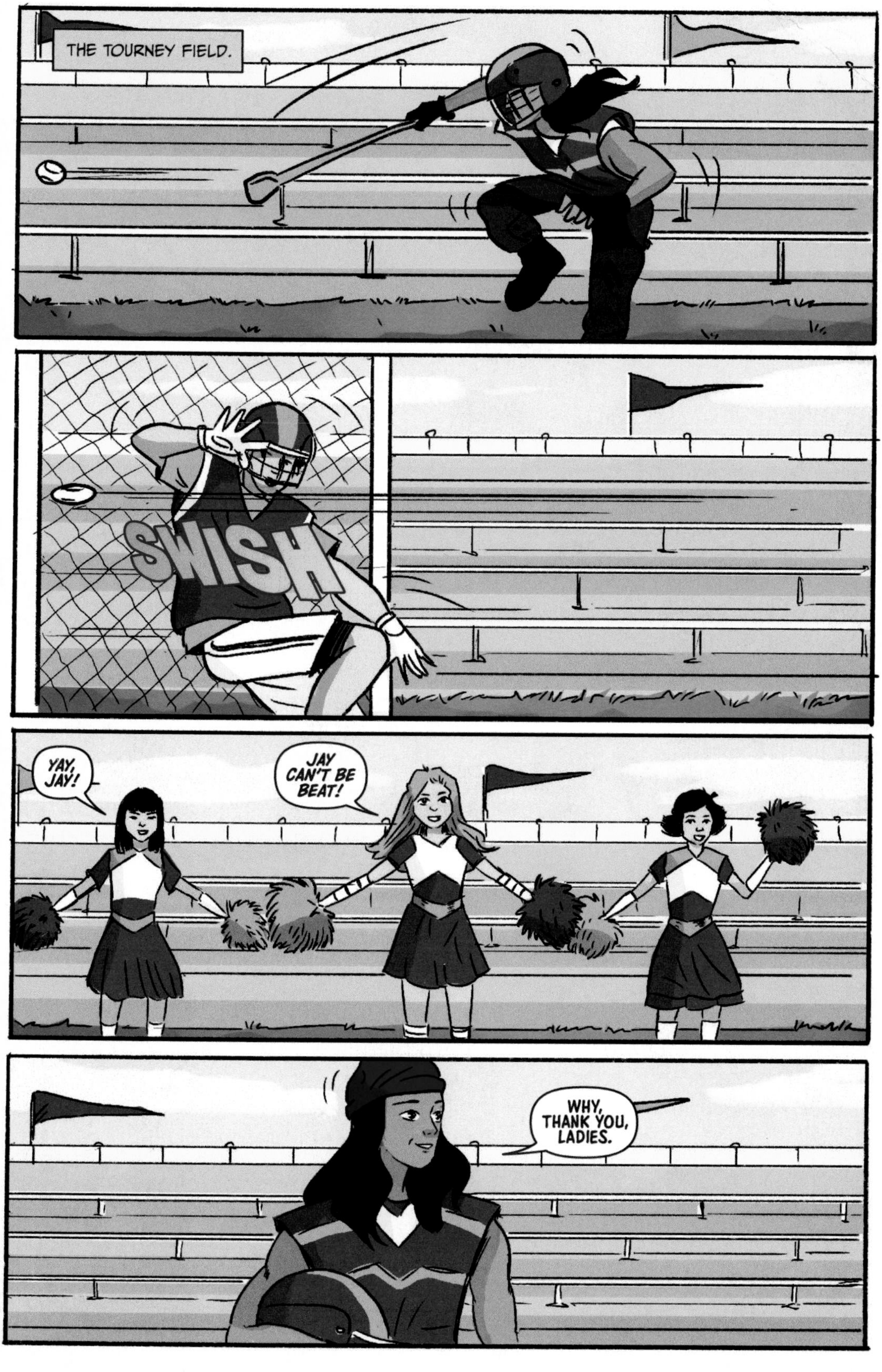
THE TOURNEY FIELD.
SWISH
YAY, JAY!
JAY CAN'T BE BEAT!
WHY, THANK YOU, LADIES.

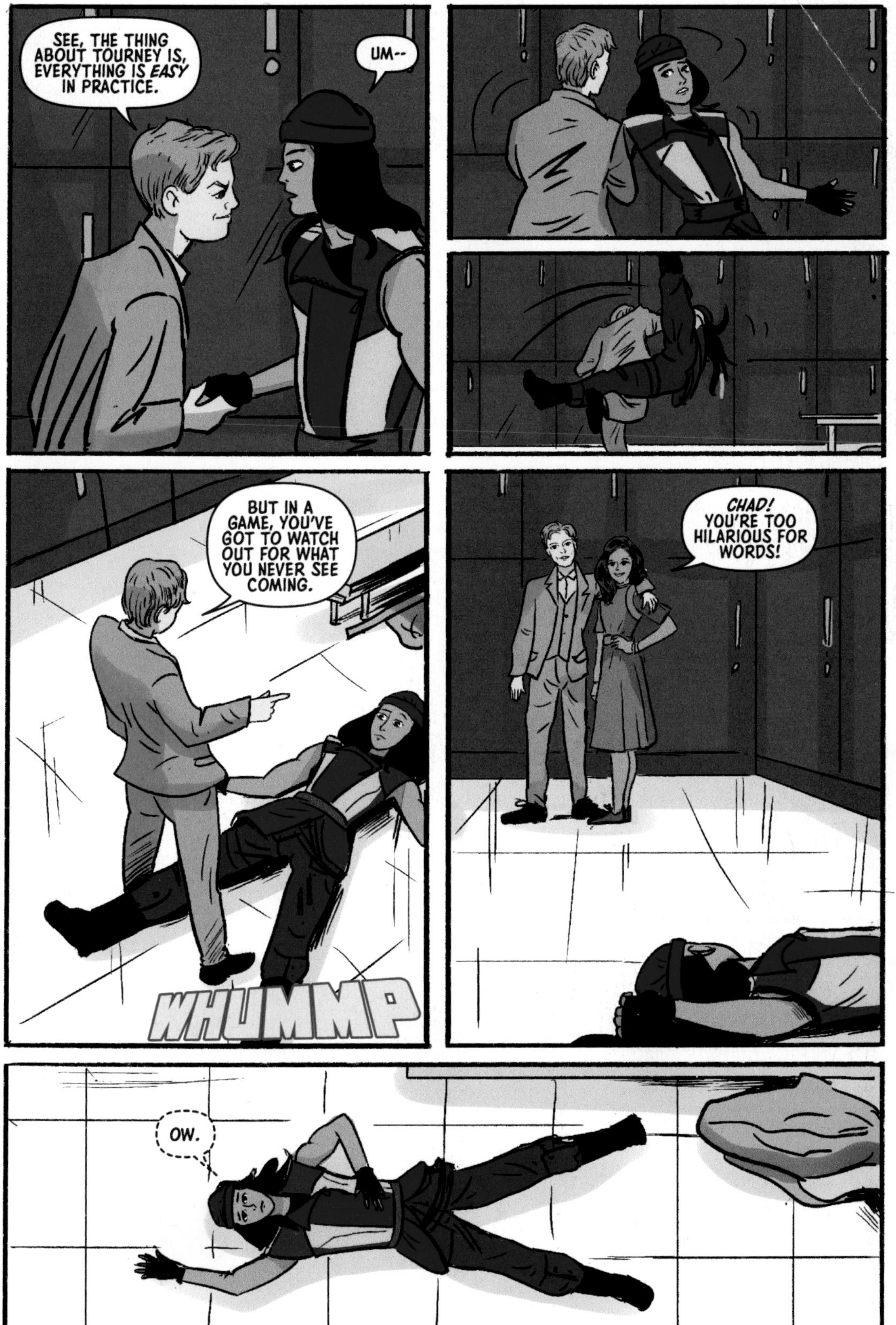
SEE, THE THING ABOUT TOURNEY IS, EVERYTHING IS *EASY* IN PRACTICE.
UM--
BUT IN A GAME, YOU'VE GOT TO WATCH OUT FOR WHAT YOU NEVER SEE COMING.
WHUMMP
CHAD! YOU'RE TOO HILARIOUS FOR WORDS!
OW.

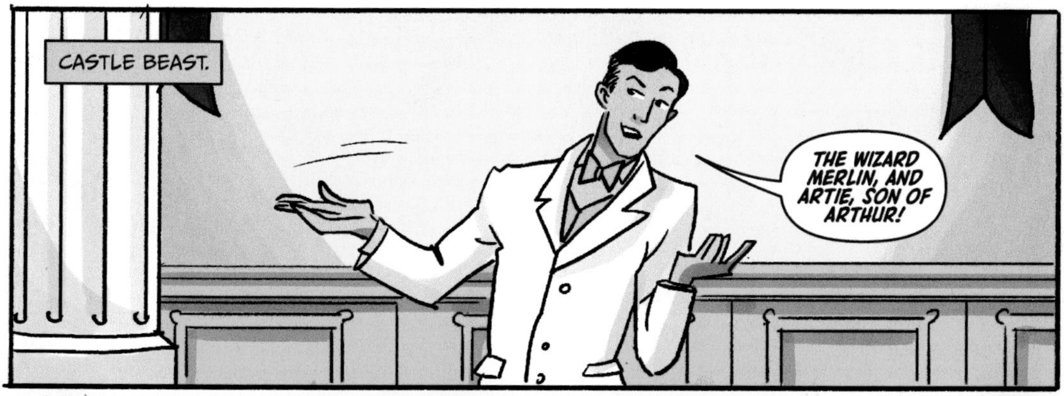
CASTLE BEAST.
THE WIZARD MERLIN, AND ARTIE, SON OF ARTHUR!

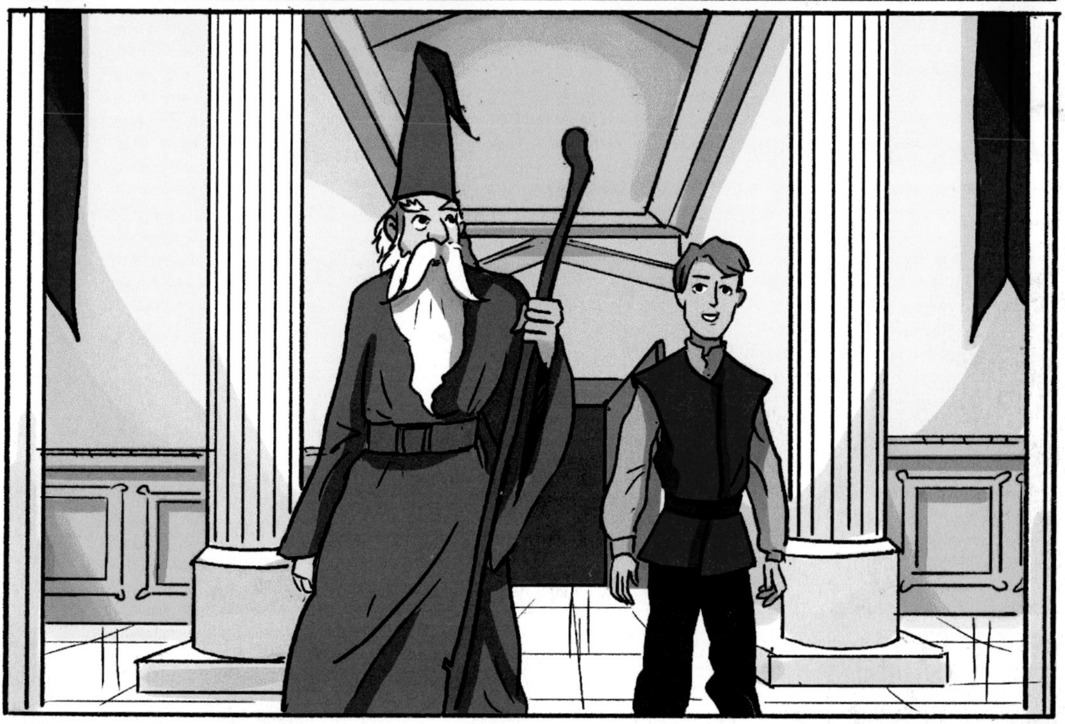

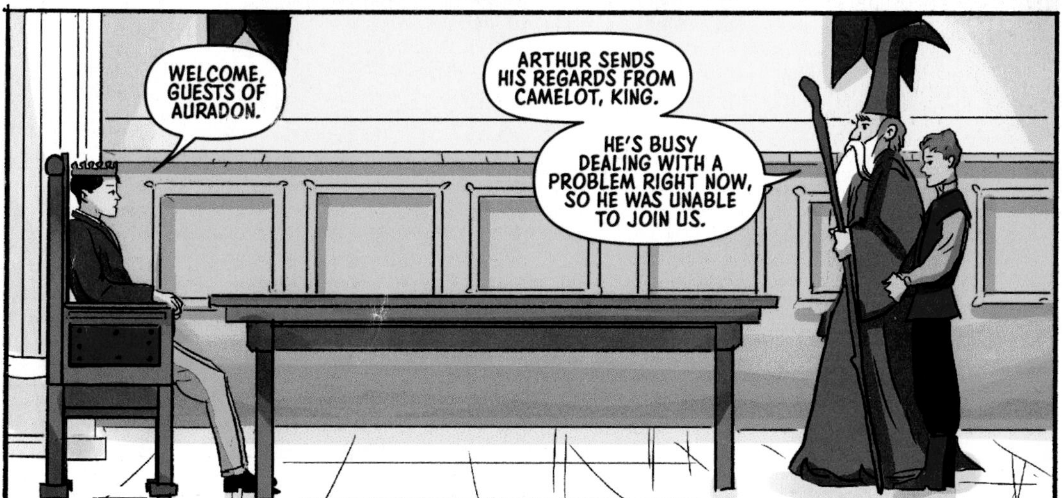
WELCOME, GUESTS OF AURADON.
ARTHUR SENDS HIS REGARDS FROM CAMELOT, KING.
HE'S BUSY DEALING WITH A PROBLEM RIGHT NOW, SO HE WAS UNABLE TO JOIN US.

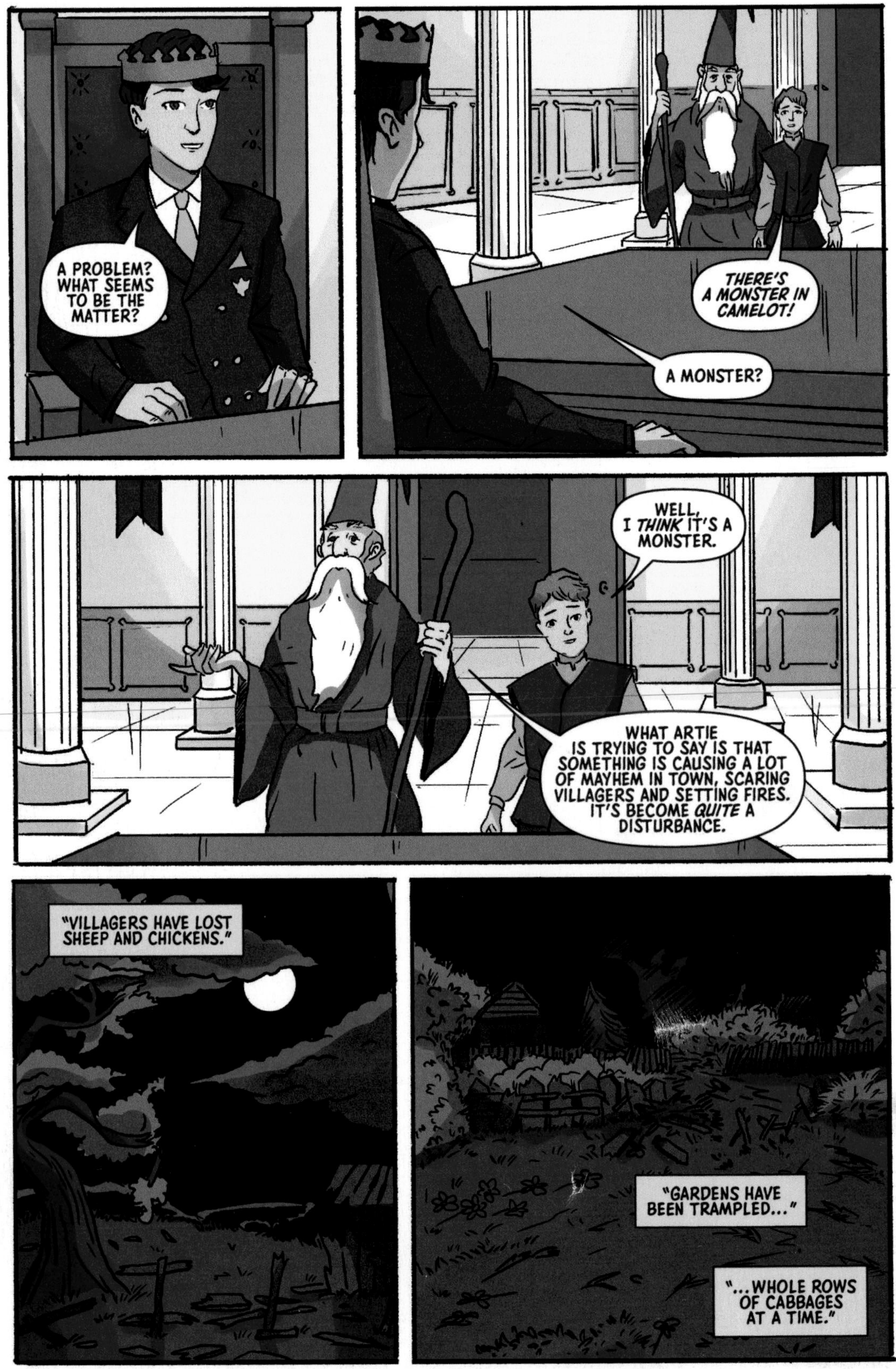
A PROBLEM? WHAT SEEMS TO BE THE MATTER?
THERE'S A MONSTER IN CAMELOT!
A MONSTER?
WELL, I THINK IT'S A MONSTER.
WHAT ARTIE IS TRYING TO SAY IS THAT SOMETHING IS CAUSING A LOT OF MAYHEM IN TOWN, SCARING VILLAGERS AND SETTING FIRES. IT'S BECOME QUITE A DISTURBANCE.
"VILLAGERS HAVE LOST SHEEP AND CHICKENS."
"GARDENS HAVE BEEN TRAMPLED..."
"...WHOLE ROWS OF CABBAGES AT A TIME."

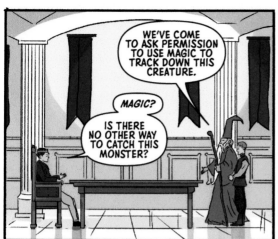

WE'VE COME TO ASK PERMISSION TO USE MAGIC TO TRACK DOWN THIS CREATURE.

MAGIC?

IS THERE NO OTHER WAY TO CATCH THIS MONSTER?

NEED I REMIND YOU THAT I AM THE WIZARD MERLIN?

I WOULDN'T BE HERE IF THERE WAS ANOTHER WAY.

I SEE....

AS THE WIZARD MERLIN, YOU KNOW VERY WELL THAT MAGIC HAS BEEN *DISCOURAGED* IN AURADON.

THE LAST TIME IT WAS USED, FAIRY GODMOTHER CREATED THE DOME THAT KEPT MAGIC OUT OF THE ISLE OF THE LOST.

AND WE'RE ALL THE BETTER FOR IT. SO FOR NOW, I AM GOING TO *REJECT* YOUR REQUEST.

BUT SIRE--!

I WILL TRAVEL TO CAMELOT MYSELF TO ASSESS THE SITUATION.

WE WILL LEAVE FIRST THING TOMORROW MORNING.

AS YOU WISH, SIRE.

LET'S HOPE CAMELOT IS STILL STANDING WHEN WE GET THERE.

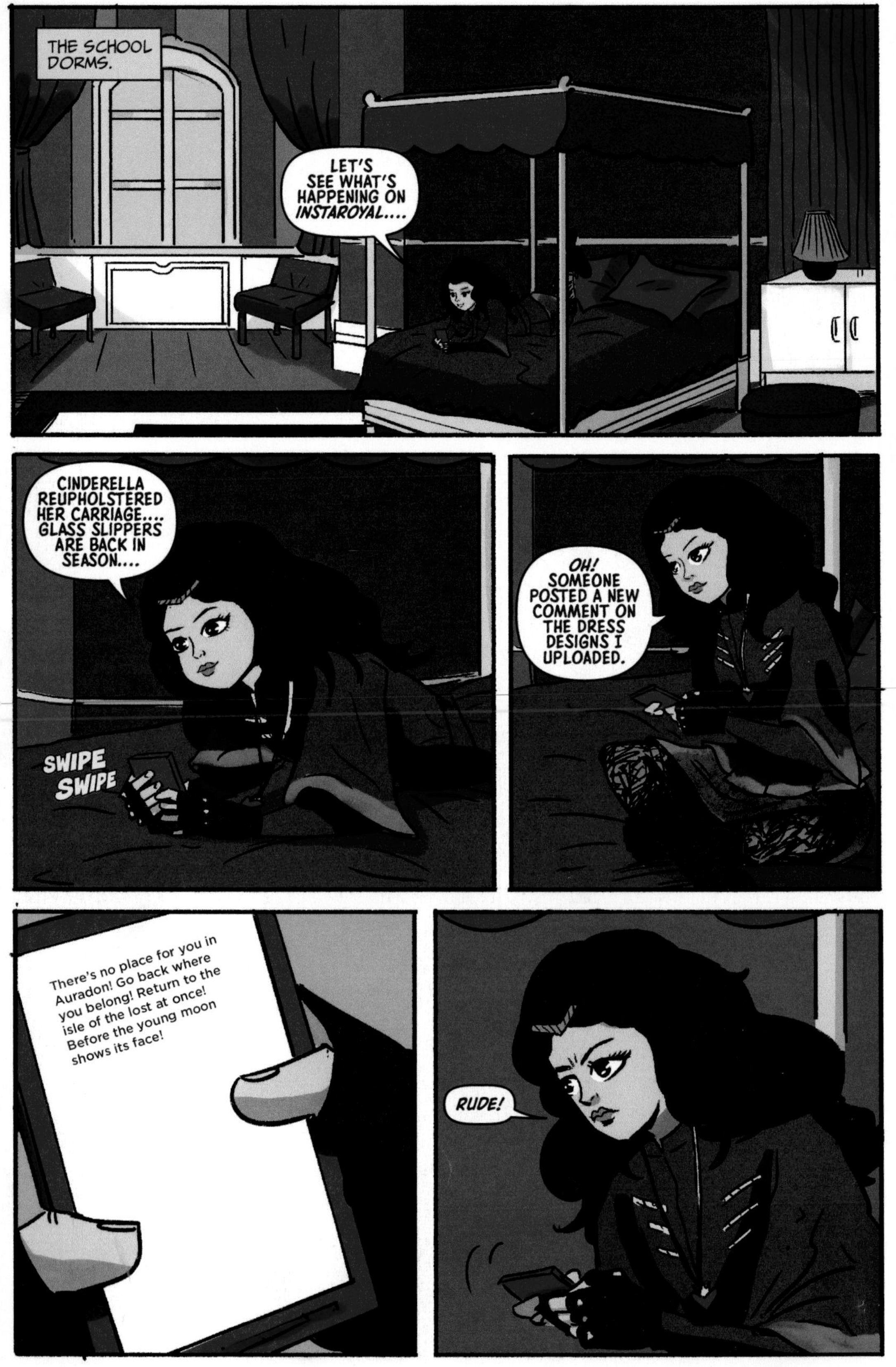
THE SCHOOL DORMS.
LET'S SEE WHAT'S HAPPENING ON *INSTAROYAL*....
CINDERELLA REUPHOLSTERED HER CARRIAGE.... GLASS SLIPPERS ARE BACK IN SEASON....
SWIPE SWIPE
OH! SOMEONE POSTED A NEW COMMENT ON THE DRESS DESIGNS I UPLOADED.
There's no place for you in Auradon! Go back where you belong! Return to the isle of the lost at once! Before the young moon shows its face!
RUDE!

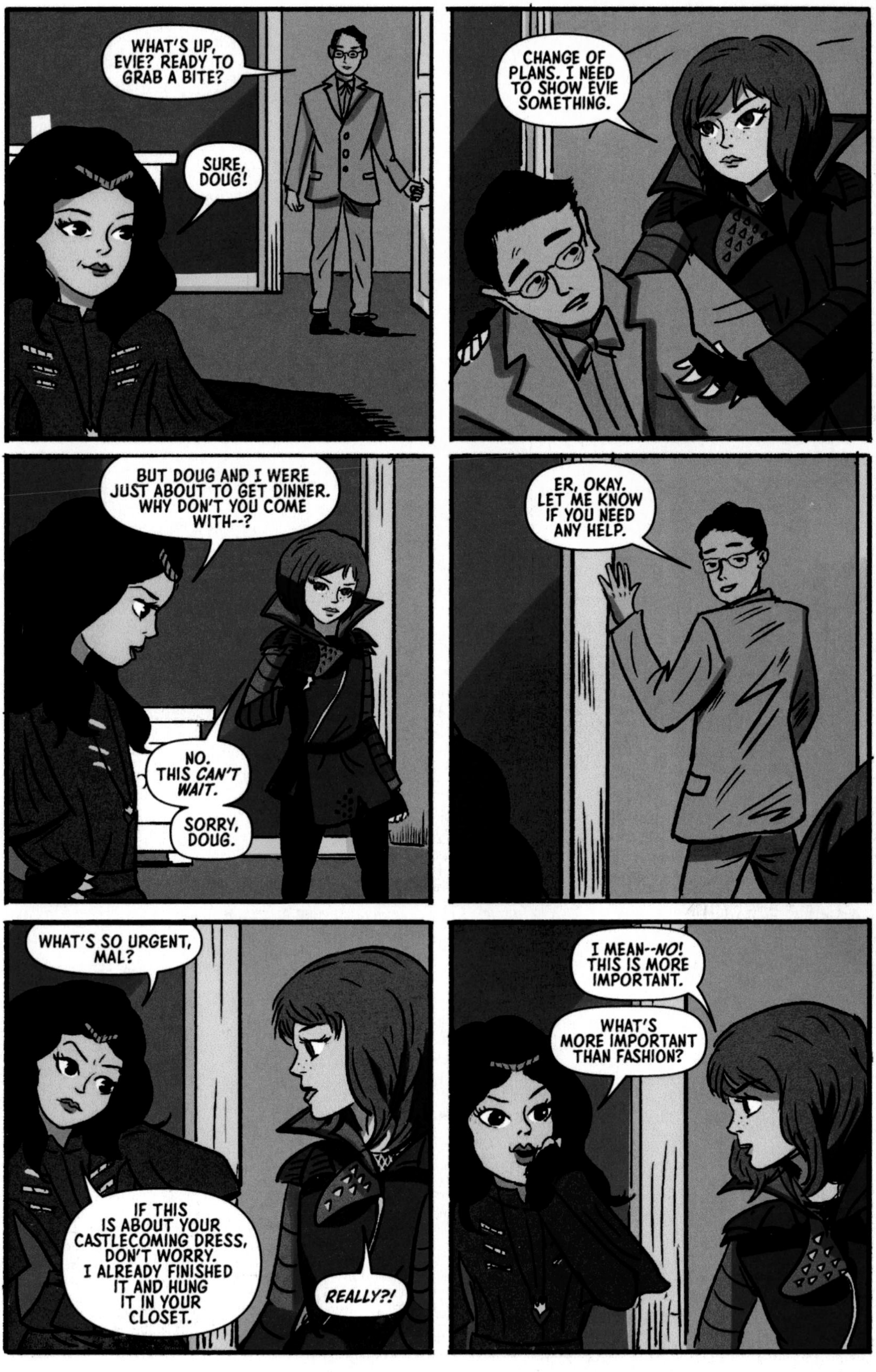
WHAT'S UP, EVIE? READY TO GRAB A BITE?
SURE, DOUG!
CHANGE OF PLANS. I NEED TO SHOW EVIE SOMETHING.
BUT DOUG AND I WERE JUST ABOUT TO GET DINNER. WHY DON'T YOU COME WITH--?
NO. THIS *CAN'T* WAIT.
SORRY, DOUG.
ER, OKAY. LET ME KNOW IF YOU NEED ANY HELP.
WHAT'S SO URGENT, MAL?
IF THIS IS ABOUT YOUR CASTLECOMING DRESS, DON'T WORRY. I ALREADY FINISHED IT AND HUNG IT IN YOUR CLOSET.
REALLY?!
I MEAN--*NO!* THIS IS MORE IMPORTANT.
WHAT'S MORE IMPORTANT THAN FASHION?

THIS.

I GOT A TEXT FROM AN UNKNOWN NUMBER. IT SAYS I HAVE TO LEAVE AURADON BEFORE THE NEXT NEW MOON.

I JUST GOT THE *SAME THING* ON MY INSTAROYAL ACCOUNT. FROM AN ANONYMOUS USER.

WHO DO YOU THINK IT IS?

MINE WAS SIGNED "M."

YOU DON'T THINK--

THAT'S *IMPOSSIBLE!* MALEFICENT IS A *LIZARD!* LIZARDS CAN'T *TYPE!*

WHO ELSE WOULD WANT US TO RETURN TO THE ISLE OF THE LOST?

THE MESSAGES HAVE TO BE FROM...

...OUR PARENTS.

ARE YOU THINKING WHAT I'M THINKING?

EVIE, WE'VE GOT TO MOVE *FAST.*

WE DON'T KNOW WHO SENT THE MESSAGES, BUT WE DO KNOW THAT OUR PARENTS WON'T REST UNTIL THEY EXACT VENGEANCE ON AURADON.

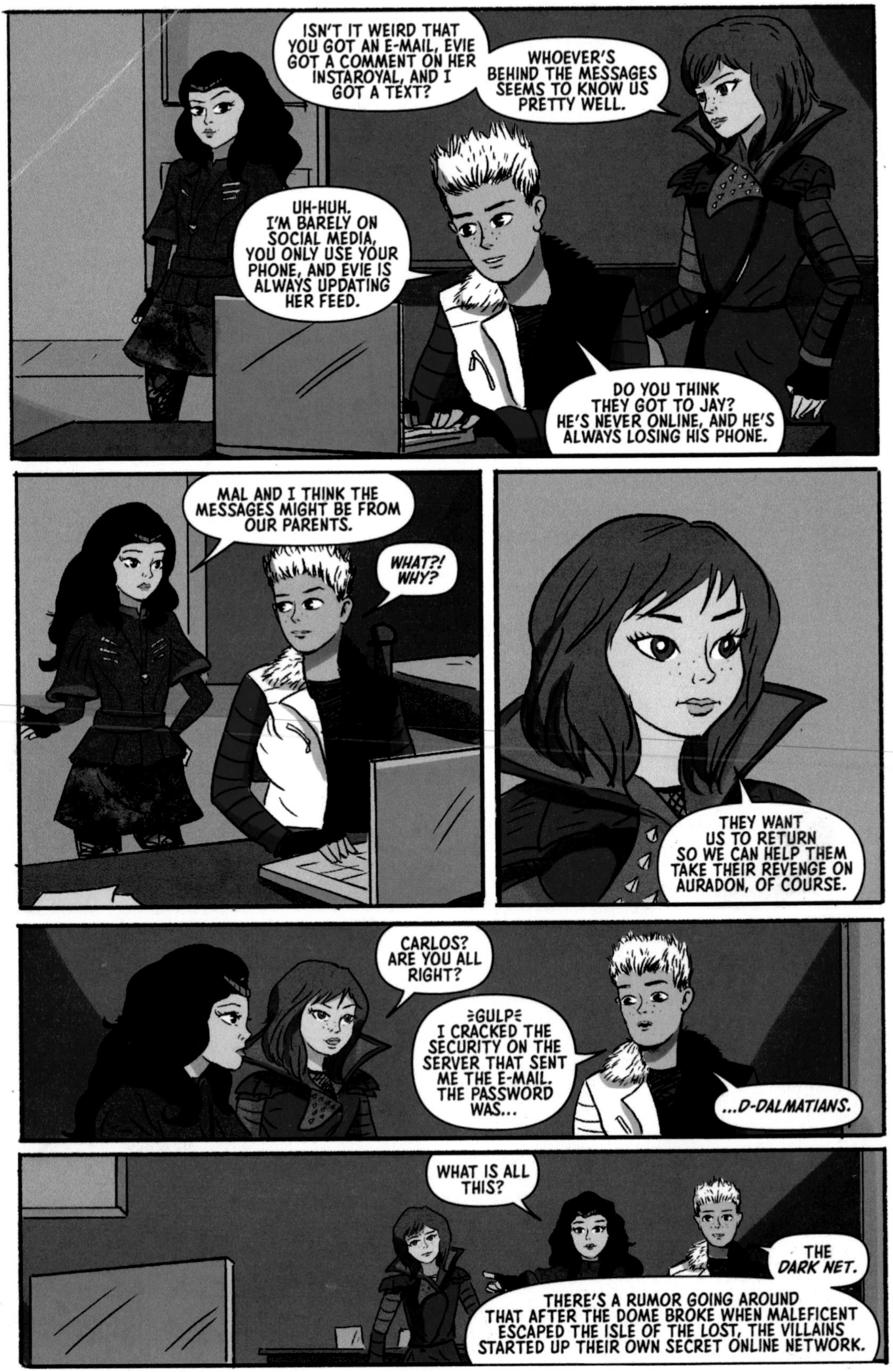

ISN'T IT WEIRD THAT YOU GOT AN E-MAIL, EVIE GOT A COMMENT ON HER INSTAROYAL, AND I GOT A TEXT?
WHOEVER'S BEHIND THE MESSAGES SEEMS TO KNOW US PRETTY WELL.
UH-HUH. I'M BARELY ON SOCIAL MEDIA, YOU ONLY USE YOUR PHONE, AND EVIE IS ALWAYS UPDATING HER FEED.
DO YOU THINK THEY GOT TO JAY? HE'S NEVER ONLINE, AND HE'S ALWAYS LOSING HIS PHONE.
MAL AND I THINK THE MESSAGES MIGHT BE FROM OUR PARENTS.
WHAT?! WHY?
THEY WANT US TO RETURN SO WE CAN HELP THEM TAKE THEIR REVENGE ON AURADON, OF COURSE.
CARLOS? ARE YOU ALL RIGHT?
GULP I CRACKED THE SECURITY ON THE SERVER THAT SENT ME THE E-MAIL. THE PASSWORD WAS...
...D-DALMATIANS.
WHAT IS ALL THIS?
THE *DARK NET*.
THERE'S A RUMOR GOING AROUND THAT AFTER THE DOME BROKE WHEN MALEFICENT ESCAPED THE ISLE OF THE LOST, THE VILLAINS STARTED UP THEIR OWN SECRET ONLINE NETWORK.

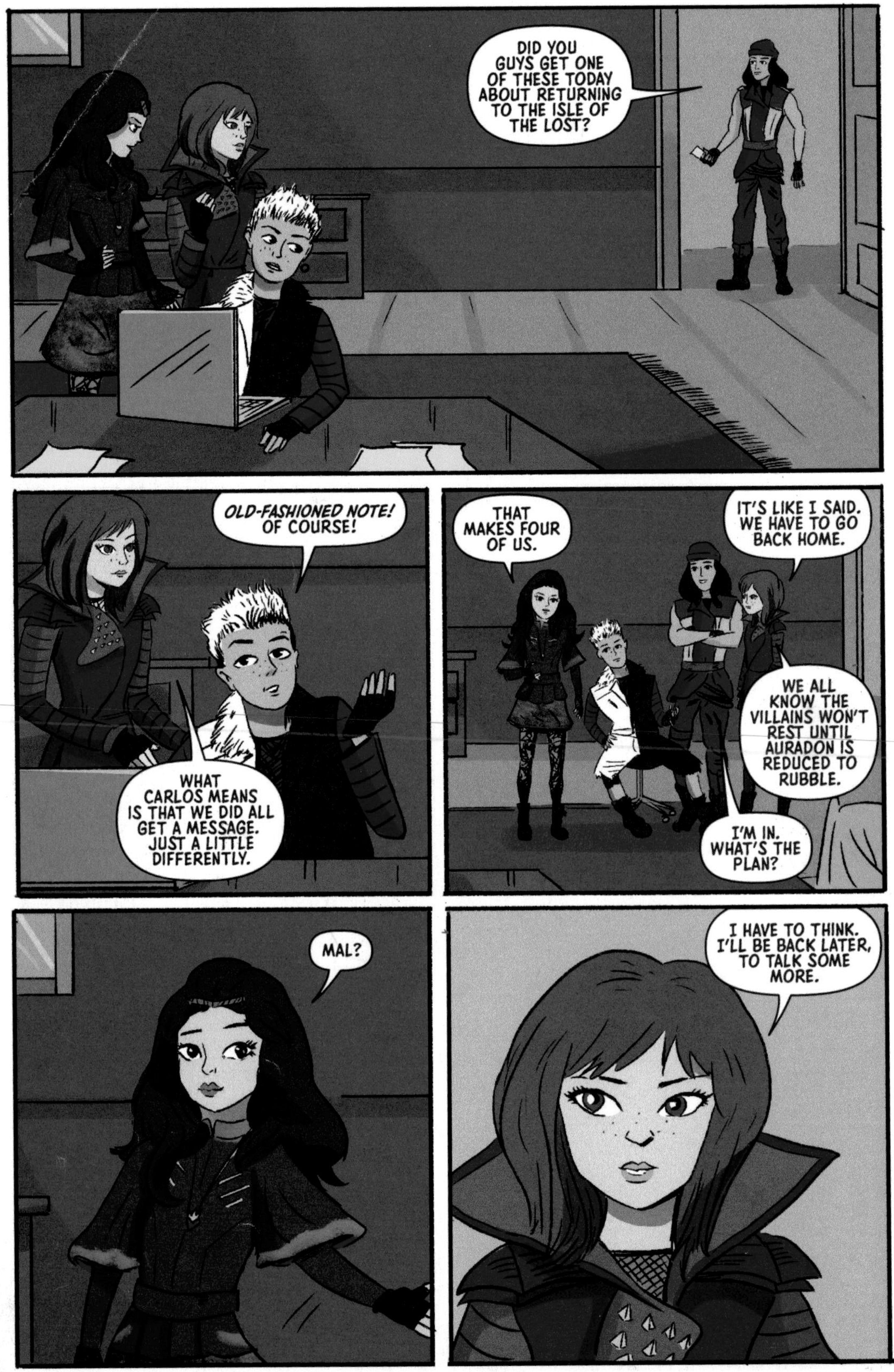
DID YOU GUYS GET ONE OF THESE TODAY ABOUT RETURNING TO THE ISLE OF THE LOST?
OLD-FASHIONED NOTE! OF COURSE!
WHAT CARLOS MEANS IS THAT WE DID ALL GET A MESSAGE. JUST A LITTLE DIFFERENTLY.
THAT MAKES FOUR OF US.
IT'S LIKE I SAID. WE HAVE TO GO BACK HOME.
WE ALL KNOW THE VILLAINS WON'T REST UNTIL AURADON IS REDUCED TO RUBBLE.
I'M IN. WHAT'S THE PLAN?
MAL?
I HAVE TO THINK. I'LL BE BACK LATER, TO TALK SOME MORE.

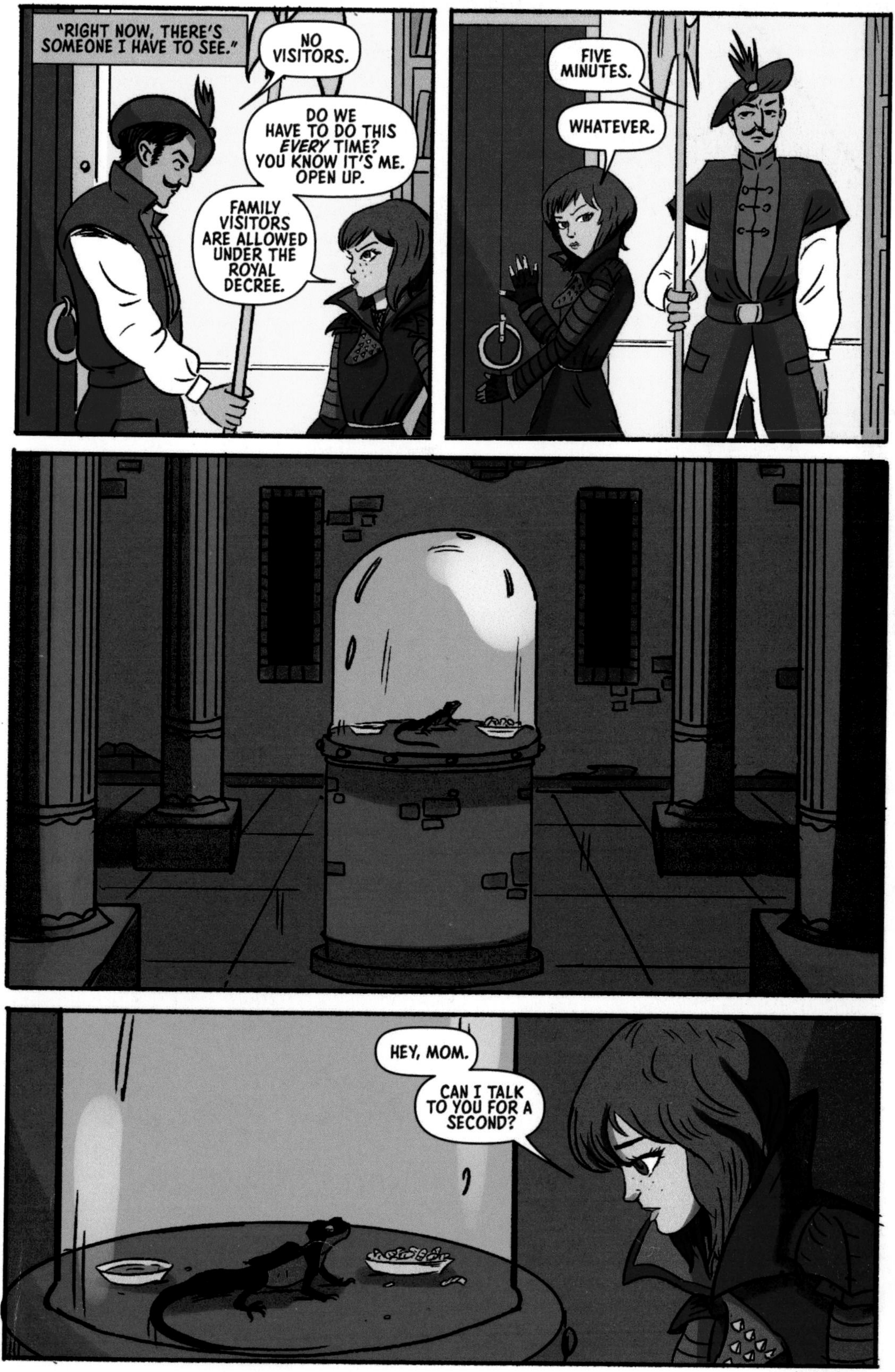
"RIGHT NOW, THERE'S SOMEONE I HAVE TO SEE."
NO VISITORS.
DO WE HAVE TO DO THIS *EVERY* TIME? YOU KNOW IT'S ME. OPEN UP.
FAMILY VISITORS ARE ALLOWED UNDER THE ROYAL DECREE.
FIVE MINUTES.
WHATEVER.
HEY, MOM.
CAN I TALK TO YOU FOR A SECOND?

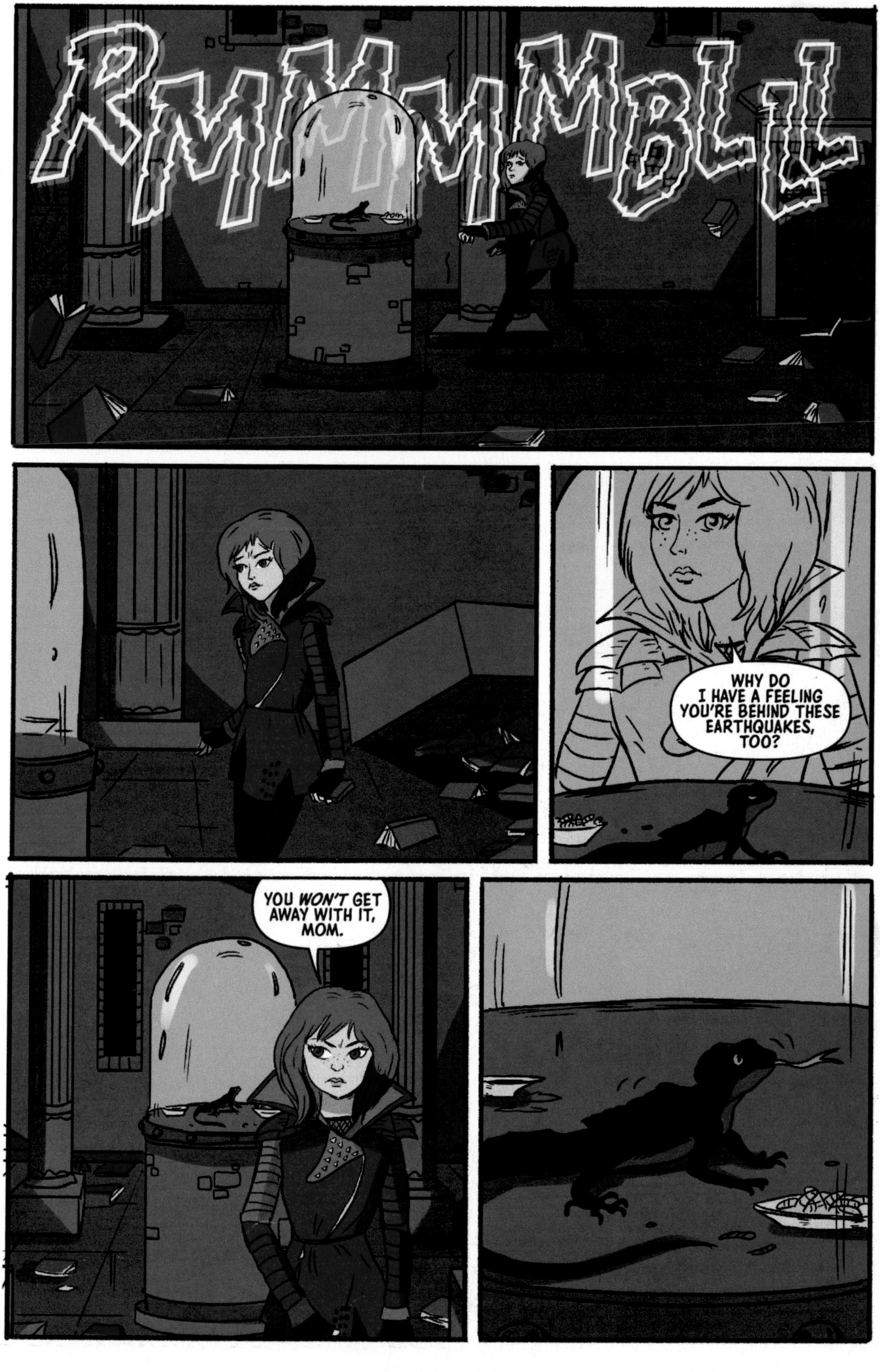
RMMMMBLLL
WHY DO I HAVE A FEELING YOU'RE BEHIND THESE EARTHQUAKES, TOO?
YOU *WON'T* GET AWAY WITH IT, MOM.

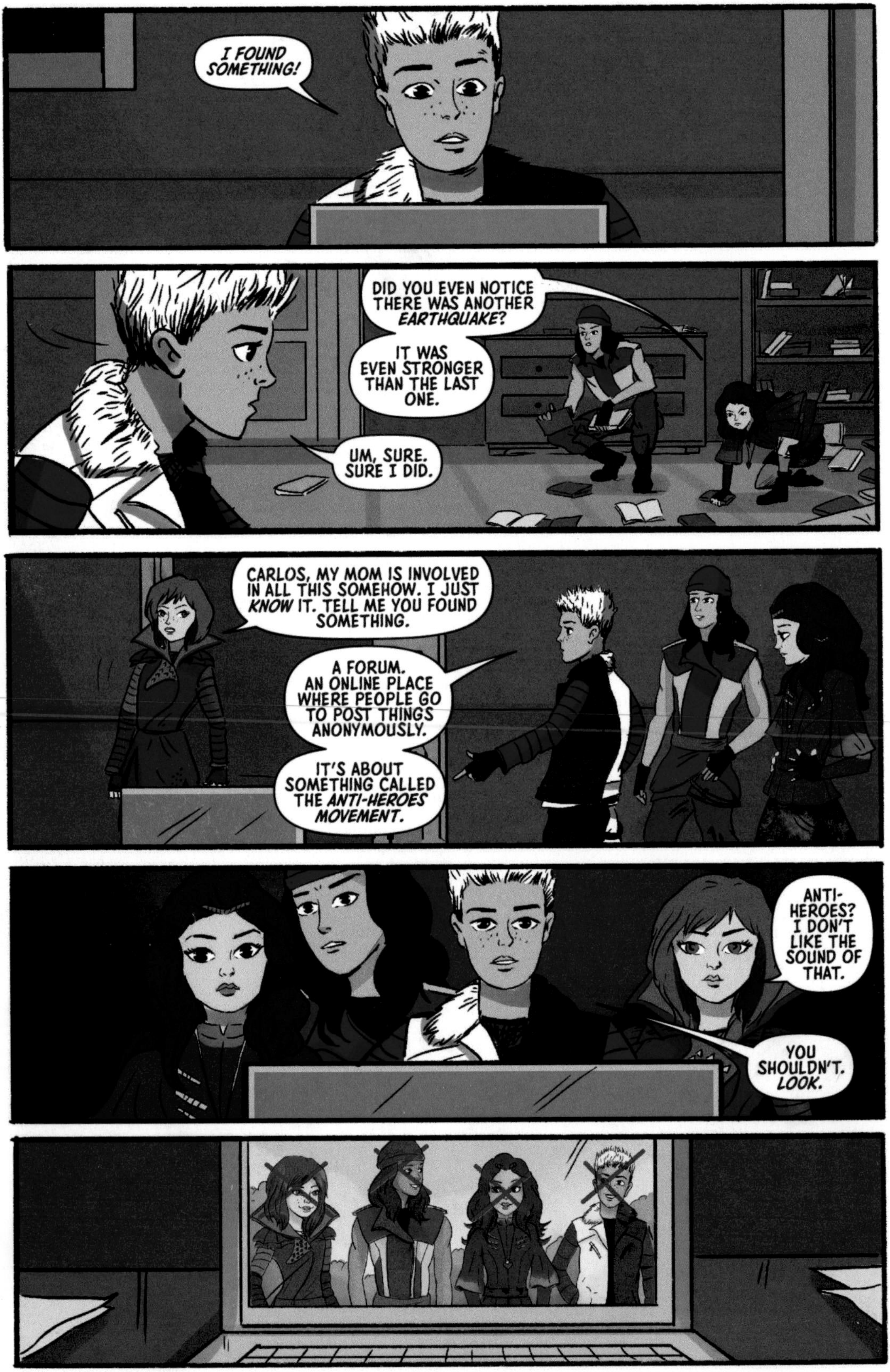
I FOUND SOMETHING!
DID YOU EVEN NOTICE THERE WAS ANOTHER *EARTHQUAKE*?
IT WAS EVEN STRONGER THAN THE LAST ONE.
UM, SURE. SURE I DID.
CARLOS, MY MOM IS INVOLVED IN ALL THIS SOMEHOW. I JUST *KNOW* IT. TELL ME YOU FOUND SOMETHING.
A FORUM. AN ONLINE PLACE WHERE PEOPLE GO TO POST THINGS ANONYMOUSLY.
IT'S ABOUT SOMETHING CALLED THE *ANTI-HEROES MOVEMENT*.
ANTI-HEROES? I DON'T LIKE THE SOUND OF THAT.
YOU SHOULDN'T. *LOOK*.

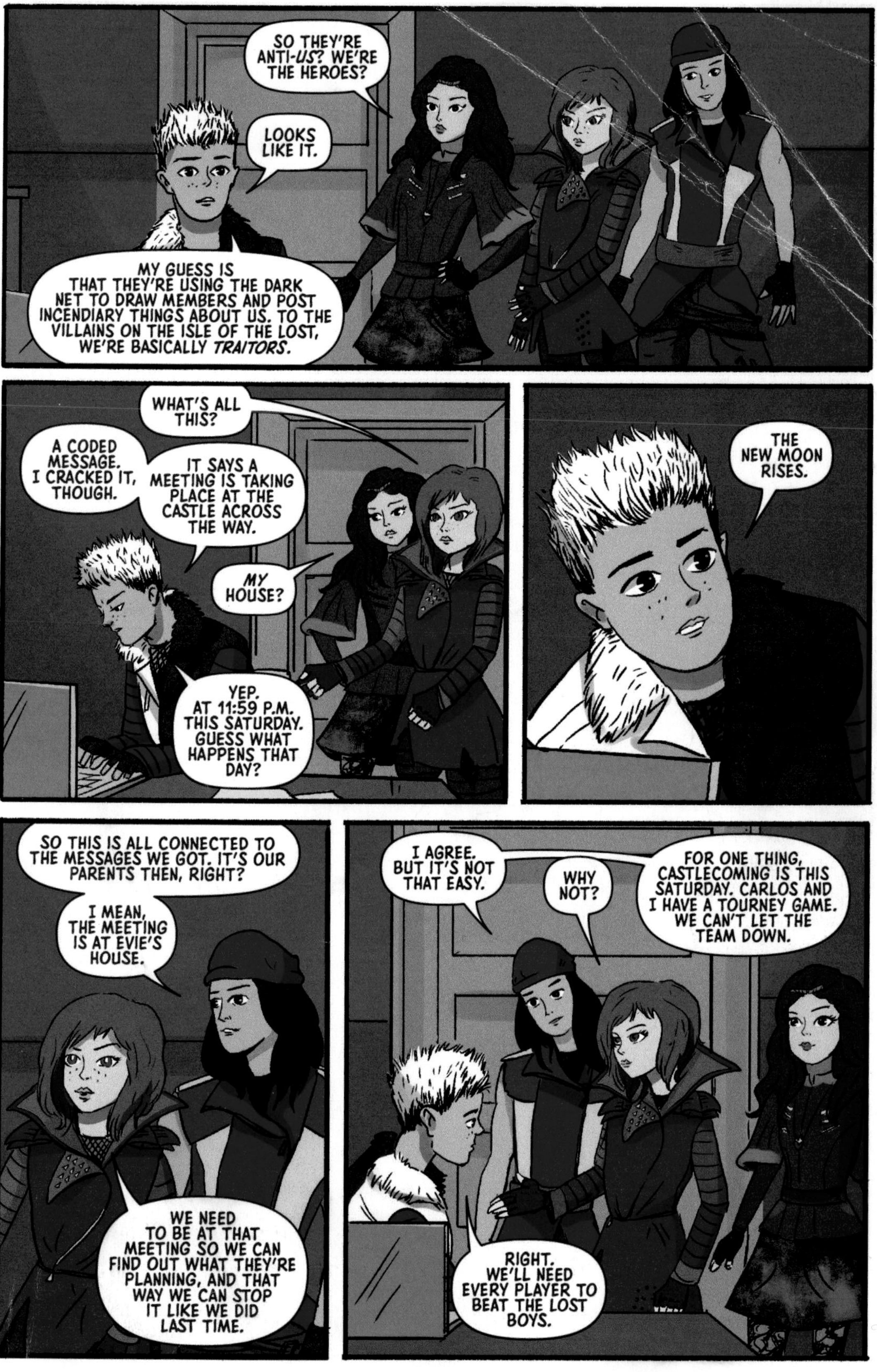
SO THEY'RE ANTI-*US*? WE'RE THE HEROES?
LOOKS LIKE IT.
MY GUESS IS THAT THEY'RE USING THE DARK NET TO DRAW MEMBERS AND POST INCENDIARY THINGS ABOUT US. TO THE VILLAINS ON THE ISLE OF THE LOST, WE'RE BASICALLY *TRAITORS*.
WHAT'S ALL THIS?
A CODED MESSAGE. I CRACKED IT, THOUGH.
IT SAYS A MEETING IS TAKING PLACE AT THE CASTLE ACROSS THE WAY.
MY HOUSE?
YEP. AT 11:59 P.M. THIS SATURDAY. GUESS WHAT HAPPENS THAT DAY?
THE NEW MOON RISES.
SO THIS IS ALL CONNECTED TO THE MESSAGES WE GOT. IT'S OUR PARENTS THEN, RIGHT?
I MEAN, THE MEETING IS AT EVIE'S HOUSE.
WE NEED TO BE AT THAT MEETING SO WE CAN FIND OUT WHAT THEY'RE PLANNING, AND THAT WAY WE CAN STOP IT LIKE WE DID LAST TIME.
I AGREE. BUT IT'S NOT THAT EASY.
WHY NOT?
FOR ONE THING, CASTLECOMING IS THIS SATURDAY. CARLOS AND I HAVE A TOURNEY GAME. WE CAN'T LET THE TEAM DOWN.
RIGHT. WE'LL NEED EVERY PLAYER TO BEAT THE LOST BOYS.

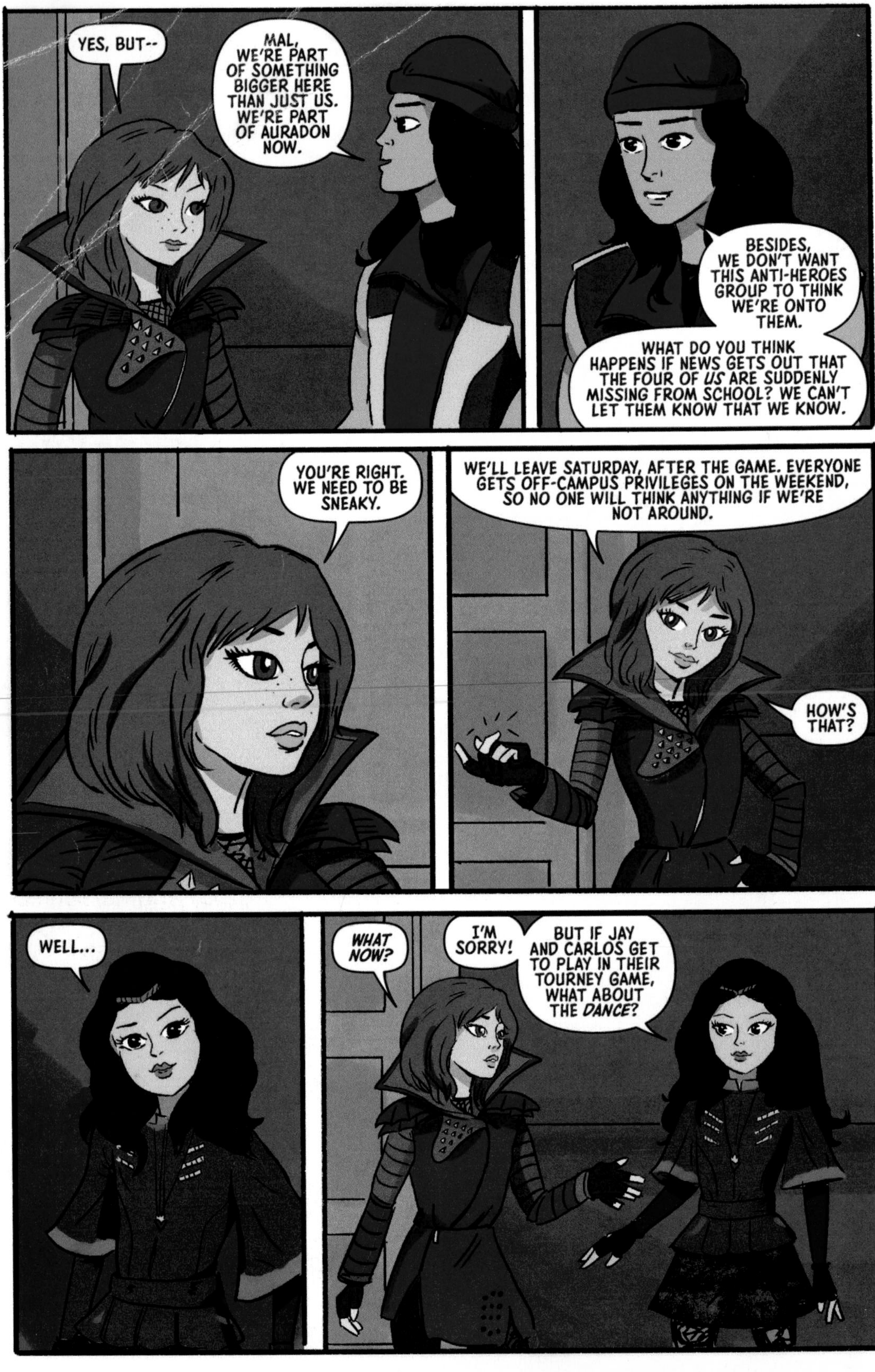
YES, BUT--
MAL, WE'RE PART OF SOMETHING BIGGER HERE THAN JUST US. WE'RE PART OF AURADON NOW.
BESIDES, WE DON'T WANT THIS ANTI-HEROES GROUP TO THINK WE'RE ONTO THEM.
WHAT DO YOU THINK HAPPENS IF NEWS GETS OUT THAT THE FOUR OF *US* ARE SUDDENLY MISSING FROM SCHOOL? WE CAN'T LET THEM KNOW THAT WE KNOW.
YOU'RE RIGHT. WE NEED TO BE SNEAKY.
WE'LL LEAVE SATURDAY, AFTER THE GAME. EVERYONE GETS OFF-CAMPUS PRIVILEGES ON THE WEEKEND, SO NO ONE WILL THINK ANYTHING IF WE'RE NOT AROUND.
HOW'S THAT?
WELL...
WHAT NOW?
I'M SORRY!
BUT IF JAY AND CARLOS GET TO PLAY IN THEIR TOURNEY GAME, WHAT ABOUT THE *DANCE*?

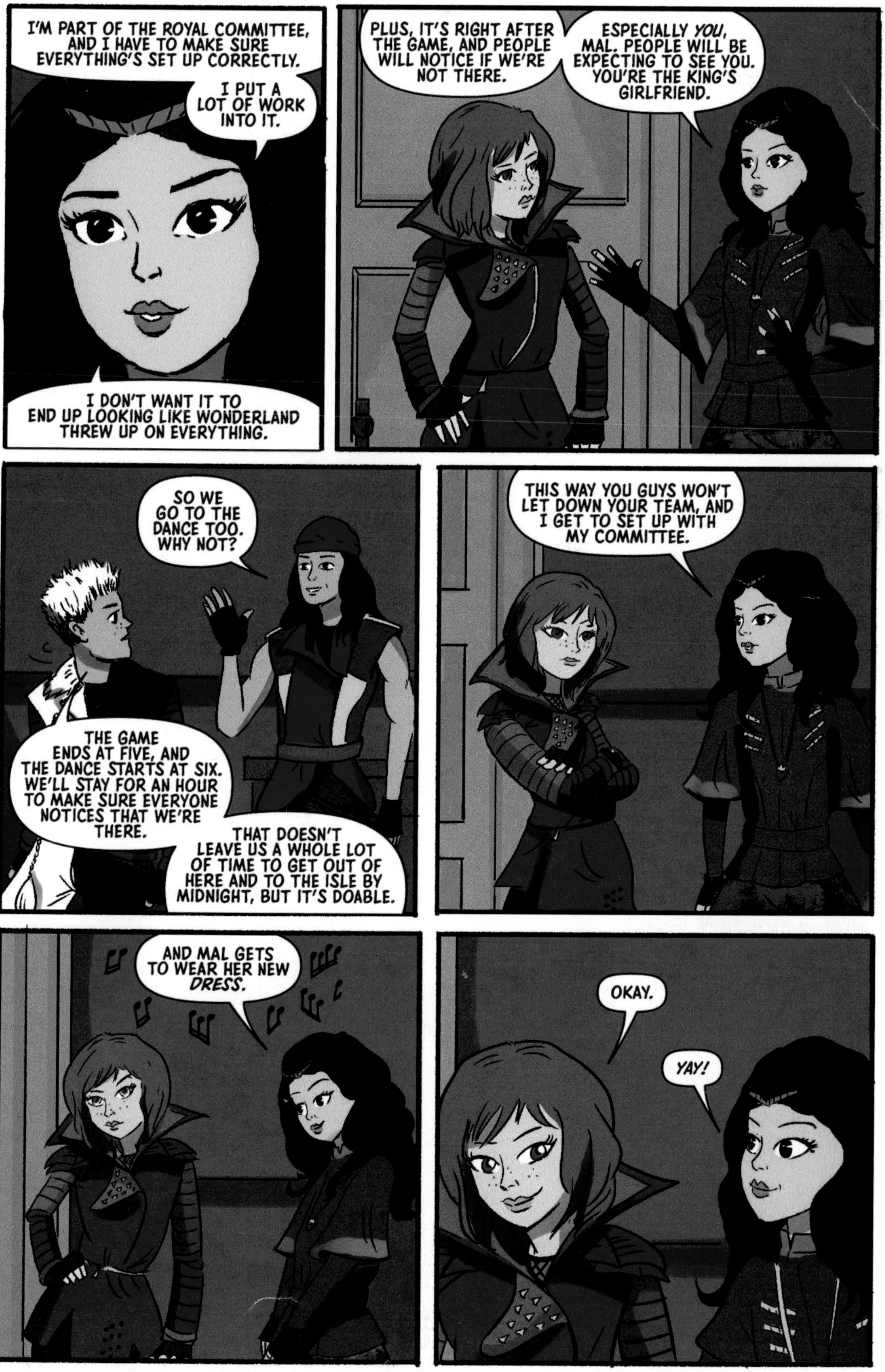
I'M PART OF THE ROYAL COMMITTEE, AND I HAVE TO MAKE SURE EVERYTHING'S SET UP CORRECTLY.
I PUT A LOT OF WORK INTO IT.
I DON'T WANT IT TO END UP LOOKING LIKE WONDERLAND THREW UP ON EVERYTHING.
PLUS, IT'S RIGHT AFTER THE GAME, AND PEOPLE WILL NOTICE IF WE'RE NOT THERE.
ESPECIALLY *YOU*, MAL. PEOPLE WILL BE EXPECTING TO SEE YOU. YOU'RE THE KING'S GIRLFRIEND.
SO WE GO TO THE DANCE TOO. WHY NOT?
THE GAME ENDS AT FIVE, AND THE DANCE STARTS AT SIX. WE'LL STAY FOR AN HOUR TO MAKE SURE EVERYONE NOTICES THAT WE'RE THERE.
THAT DOESN'T LEAVE US A WHOLE LOT OF TIME TO GET OUT OF HERE AND TO THE ISLE BY MIDNIGHT, BUT IT'S DOABLE.
THIS WAY YOU GUYS WON'T LET DOWN YOUR TEAM, AND I GET TO SET UP WITH MY COMMITTEE.
AND MAL GETS TO WEAR HER NEW *DRESS*.
OKAY.
YAY!

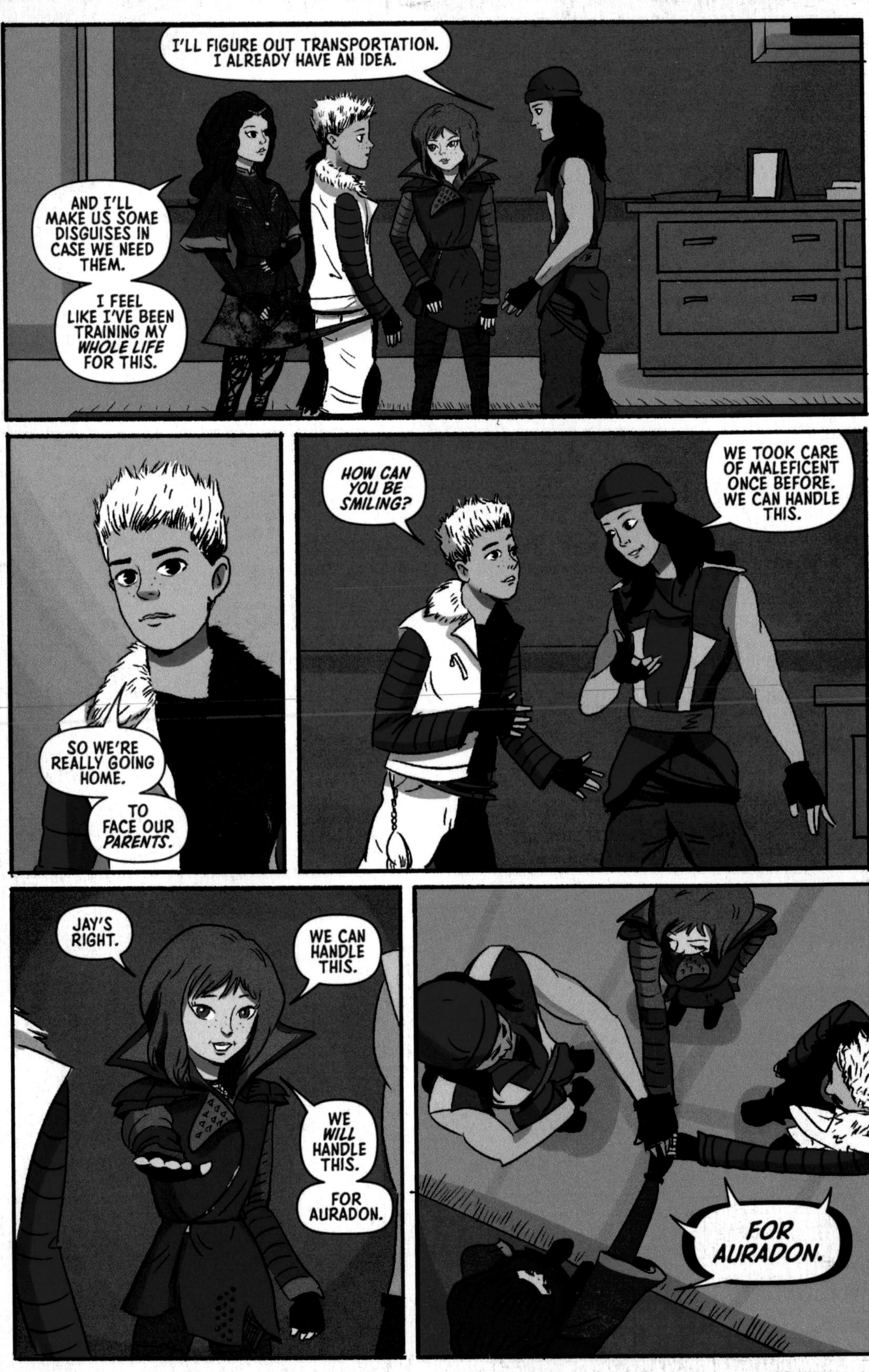
I'LL FIGURE OUT TRANSPORTATION. I ALREADY HAVE AN IDEA.
AND I'LL MAKE US SOME DISGUISES IN CASE WE NEED THEM.
I FEEL LIKE I'VE BEEN TRAINING MY *WHOLE LIFE* FOR THIS.
SO WE'RE REALLY GOING HOME.
TO FACE OUR *PARENTS*.
HOW CAN YOU BE SMILING?
WE TOOK CARE OF MALEFICENT ONCE BEFORE. WE CAN HANDLE THIS.
JAY'S RIGHT.
WE CAN HANDLE THIS.
WE *WILL* HANDLE THIS.
FOR AURADON.
FOR AURADON.

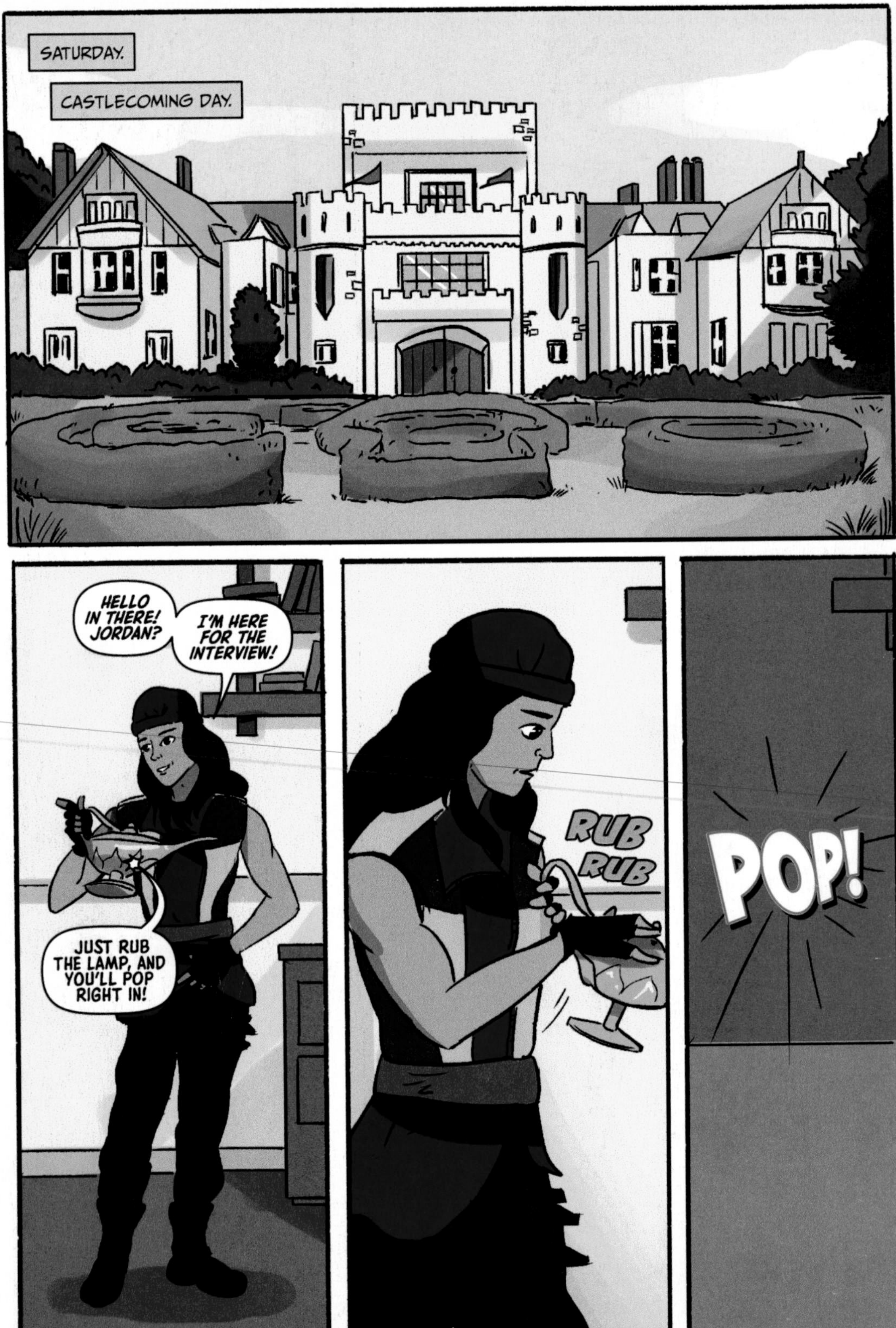
SATURDAY.
CASTLECOMING DAY.
HELLO IN THERE! JORDAN?
I'M HERE FOR THE INTERVIEW!
JUST RUB THE LAMP, AND YOU'LL POP RIGHT IN!
RUB RUB
POP!

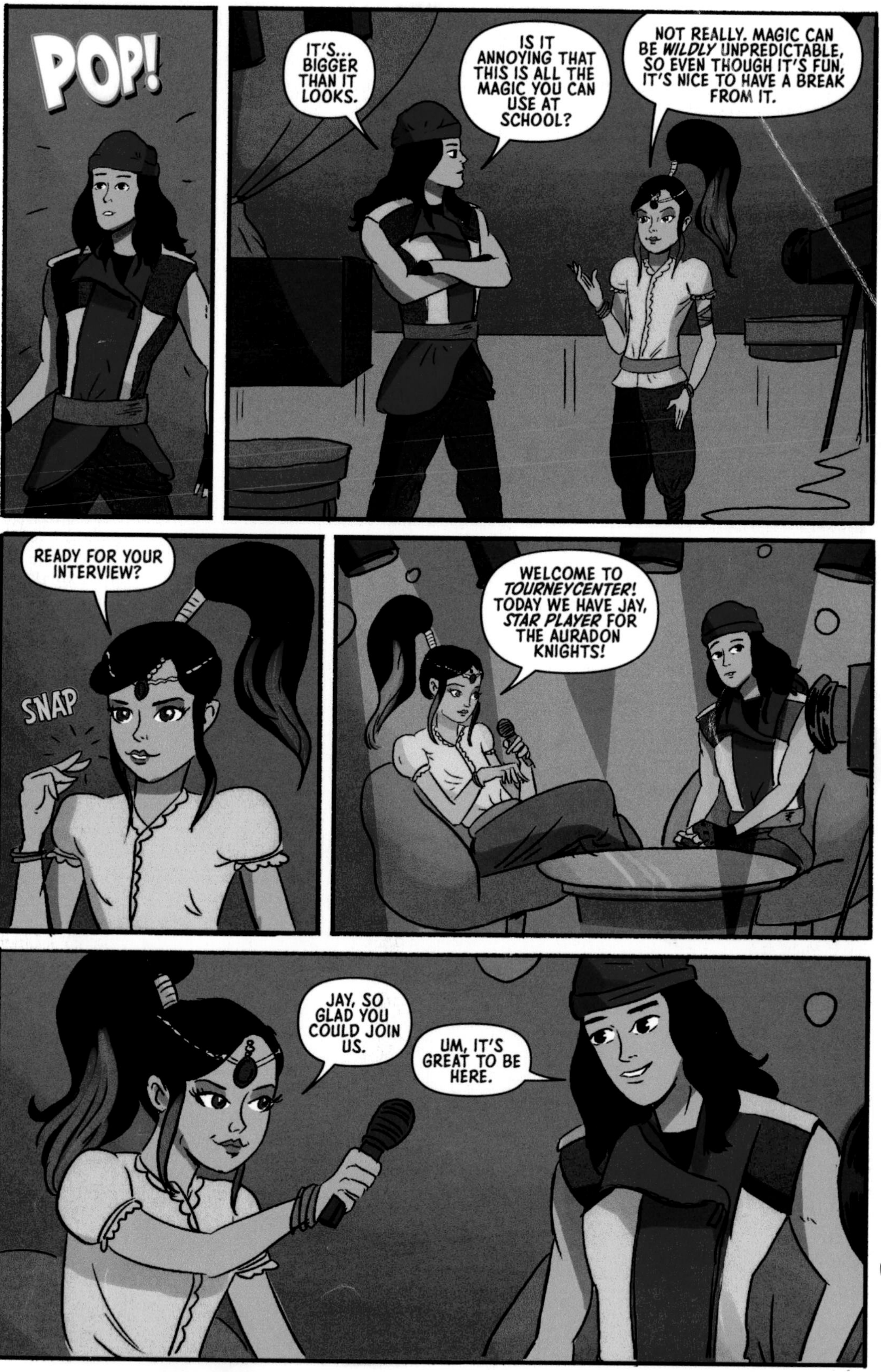
POP!
IT'S... BIGGER THAN IT LOOKS.
IS IT ANNOYING THAT THIS IS ALL THE MAGIC YOU CAN USE AT SCHOOL?
NOT REALLY. MAGIC CAN BE *WILDLY* UNPREDICTABLE, SO EVEN THOUGH IT'S FUN, IT'S NICE TO HAVE A BREAK FROM IT.
READY FOR YOUR INTERVIEW?
SNAP
WELCOME TO *TOURNEYCENTER*! TODAY WE HAVE JAY, *STAR PLAYER* FOR THE AURADON KNIGHTS!
JAY, SO GLAD YOU COULD JOIN US.
UM, IT'S GREAT TO BE HERE.

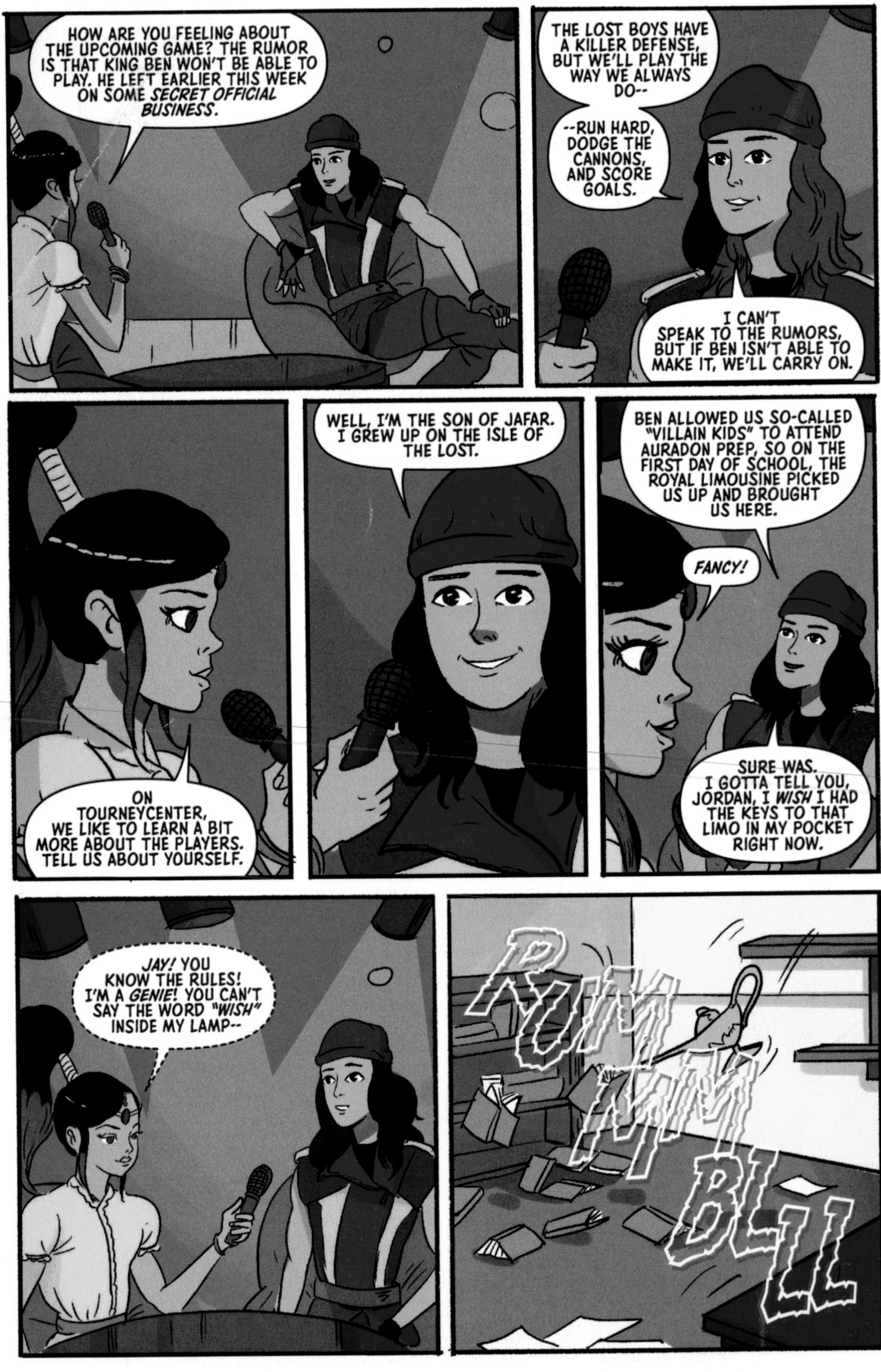

HOW ARE YOU FEELING ABOUT THE UPCOMING GAME? THE RUMOR IS THAT KING BEN WON'T BE ABLE TO PLAY. HE LEFT EARLIER THIS WEEK ON SOME *SECRET OFFICIAL BUSINESS*.
THE LOST BOYS HAVE A KILLER DEFENSE, BUT WE'LL PLAY THE WAY WE ALWAYS DO--
--RUN HARD, DODGE THE CANNONS, AND SCORE GOALS.
I CAN'T SPEAK TO THE RUMORS, BUT IF BEN ISN'T ABLE TO MAKE IT, WE'LL CARRY ON.
ON TOURNEYCENTER, WE LIKE TO LEARN A BIT MORE ABOUT THE PLAYERS. TELL US ABOUT YOURSELF.
WELL, I'M THE SON OF JAFAR. I GREW UP ON THE ISLE OF THE LOST.
BEN ALLOWED US *SO-CALLED* "*VILLAIN KIDS*" TO ATTEND AURADON PREP, SO ON THE FIRST DAY OF SCHOOL, THE ROYAL LIMOUSINE PICKED US UP AND BROUGHT US HERE.
FANCY!
SURE WAS. I GOTTA TELL YOU, JORDAN, I *WISH* I HAD THE KEYS TO THAT LIMO IN MY POCKET RIGHT NOW.
JAY! YOU KNOW THE RULES! I'M A *GENIE*! YOU CAN'T SAY THE WORD *"WISH"* INSIDE MY LAMP--
RUMMMBLLL

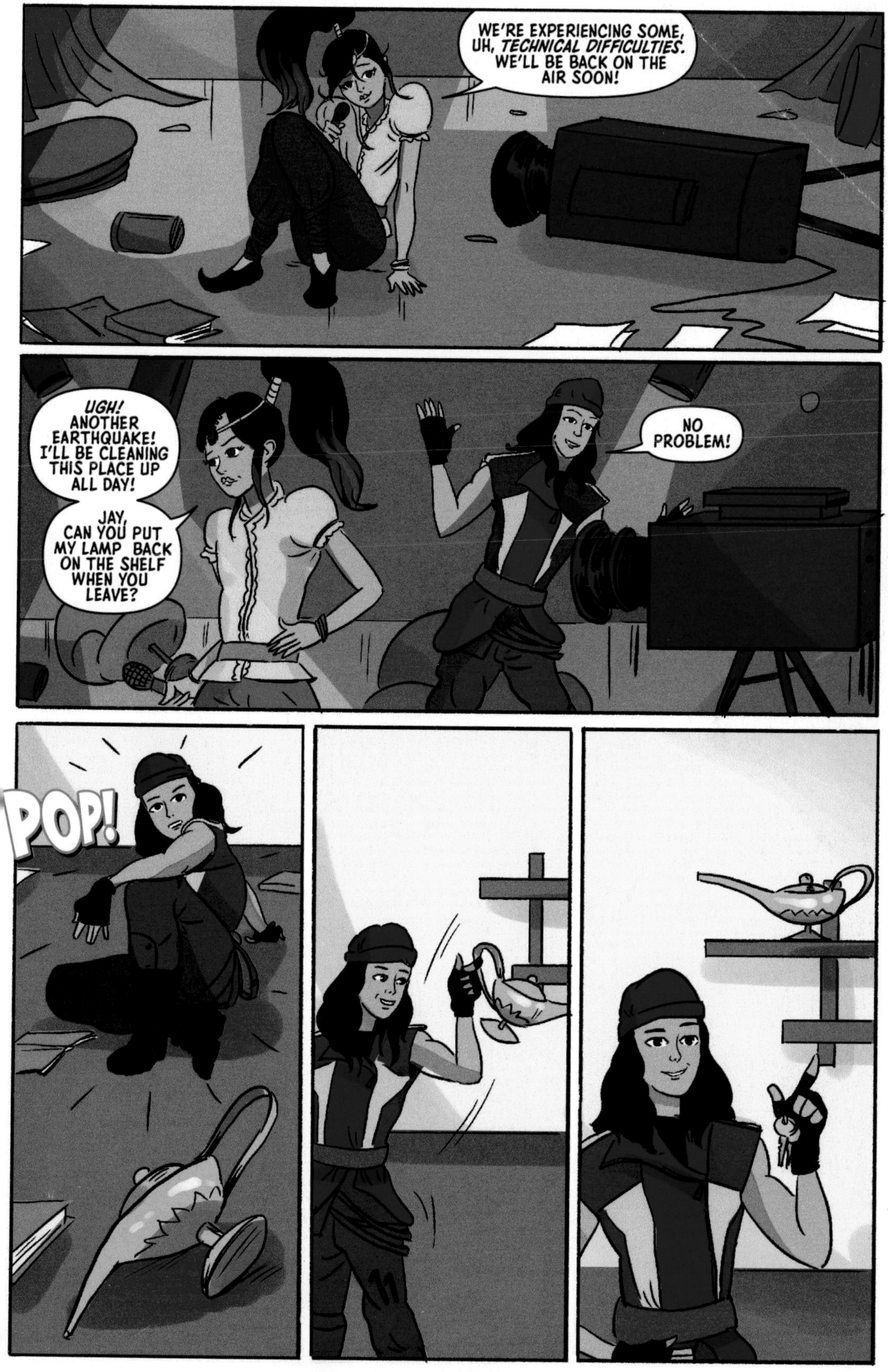
WE'RE EXPERIENCING SOME, UH, *TECHNICAL DIFFICULTIES*. WE'LL BE BACK ON THE AIR SOON!
UGH! ANOTHER EARTHQUAKE! I'LL BE CLEANING THIS PLACE UP ALL DAY!
JAY, CAN YOU PUT MY LAMP BACK ON THE SHELF WHEN YOU LEAVE?
NO PROBLEM!
POP!

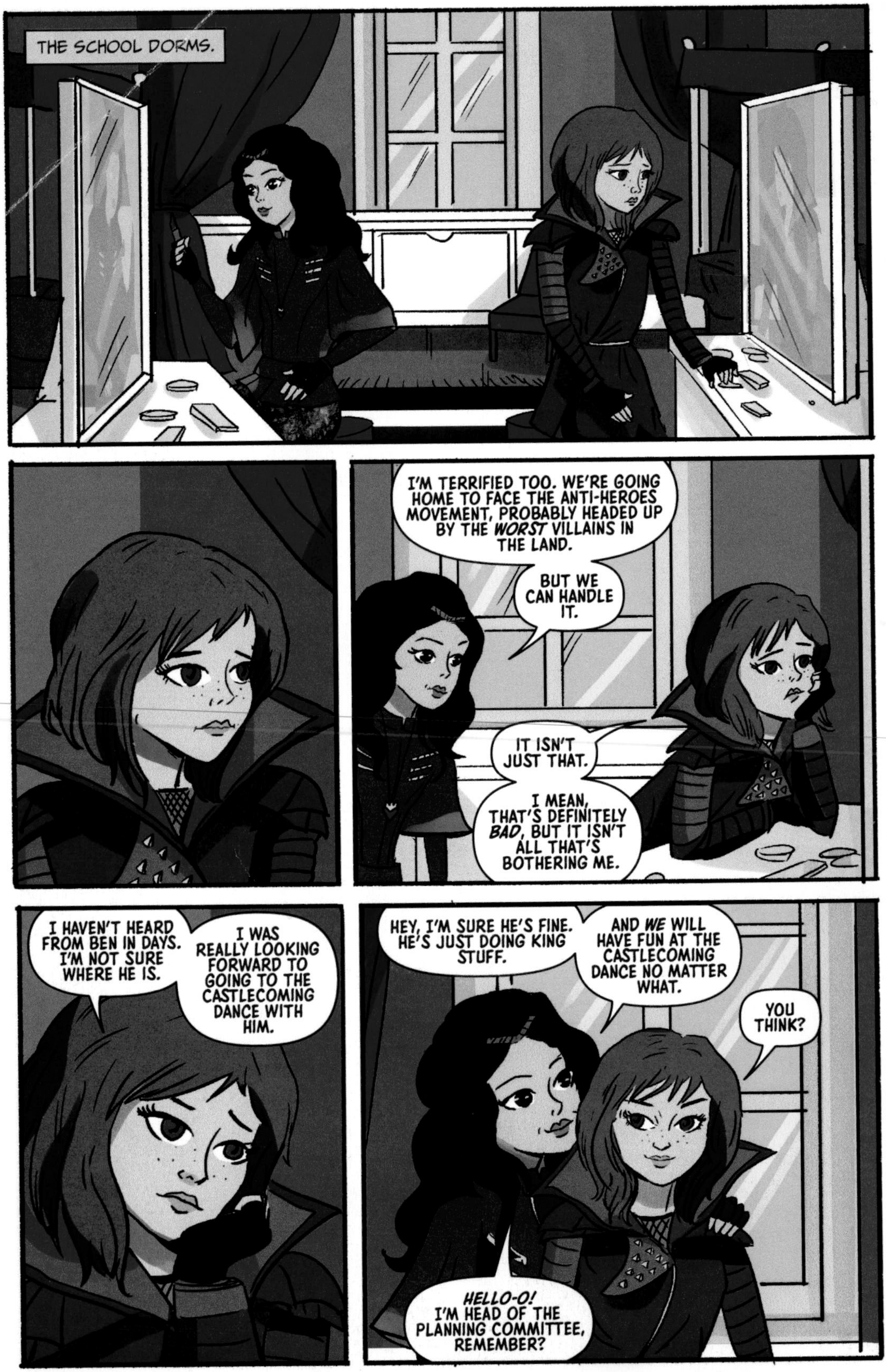
THE SCHOOL DORMS.
I'M TERRIFIED TOO. WE'RE GOING HOME TO FACE THE ANTI-HEROES MOVEMENT, PROBABLY HEADED UP BY THE *WORST* VILLAINS IN THE LAND.
BUT WE CAN HANDLE IT.
IT ISN'T JUST THAT.
I MEAN, THAT'S DEFINITELY *BAD*, BUT IT ISN'T ALL THAT'S BOTHERING ME.
I HAVEN'T HEARD FROM BEN IN DAYS. I'M NOT SURE WHERE HE IS.
I WAS REALLY LOOKING FORWARD TO GOING TO THE CASTLECOMING DANCE WITH HIM.
HEY, I'M SURE HE'S FINE. HE'S JUST DOING KING STUFF.
AND *WE* WILL HAVE FUN AT THE CASTLECOMING DANCE NO MATTER WHAT.
YOU THINK?
HELLO-O! I'M HEAD OF THE PLANNING COMMITTEE, REMEMBER?

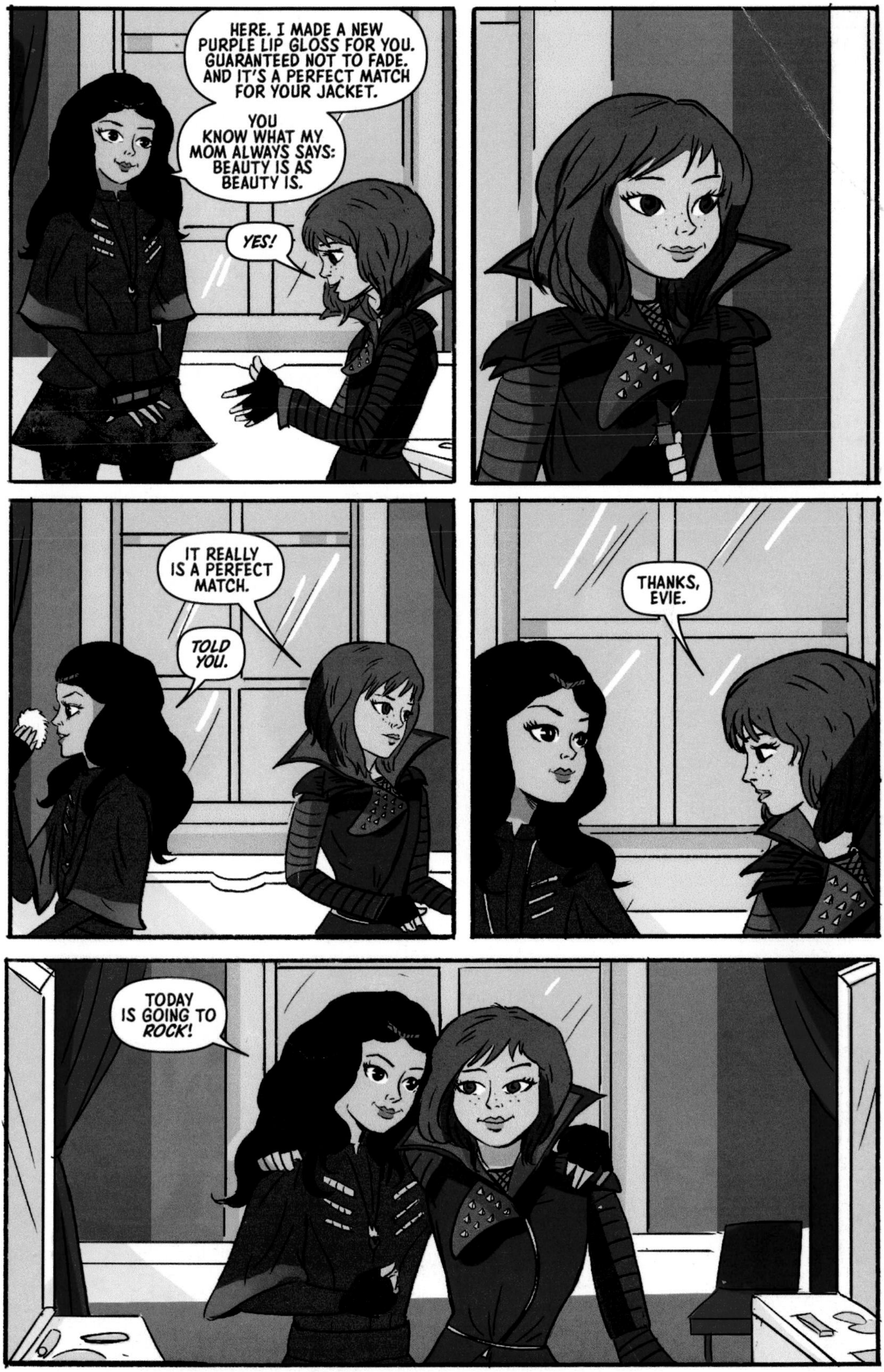
HERE. I MADE A NEW PURPLE LIP GLOSS FOR YOU. GUARANTEED NOT TO FADE. AND IT'S A PERFECT MATCH FOR YOUR JACKET.
YOU KNOW WHAT MY MOM ALWAYS SAYS: BEAUTY IS AS BEAUTY IS.
YES!
IT REALLY IS A PERFECT MATCH.
TOLD YOU.
THANKS, EVIE.
TODAY IS GOING TO *ROCK*!

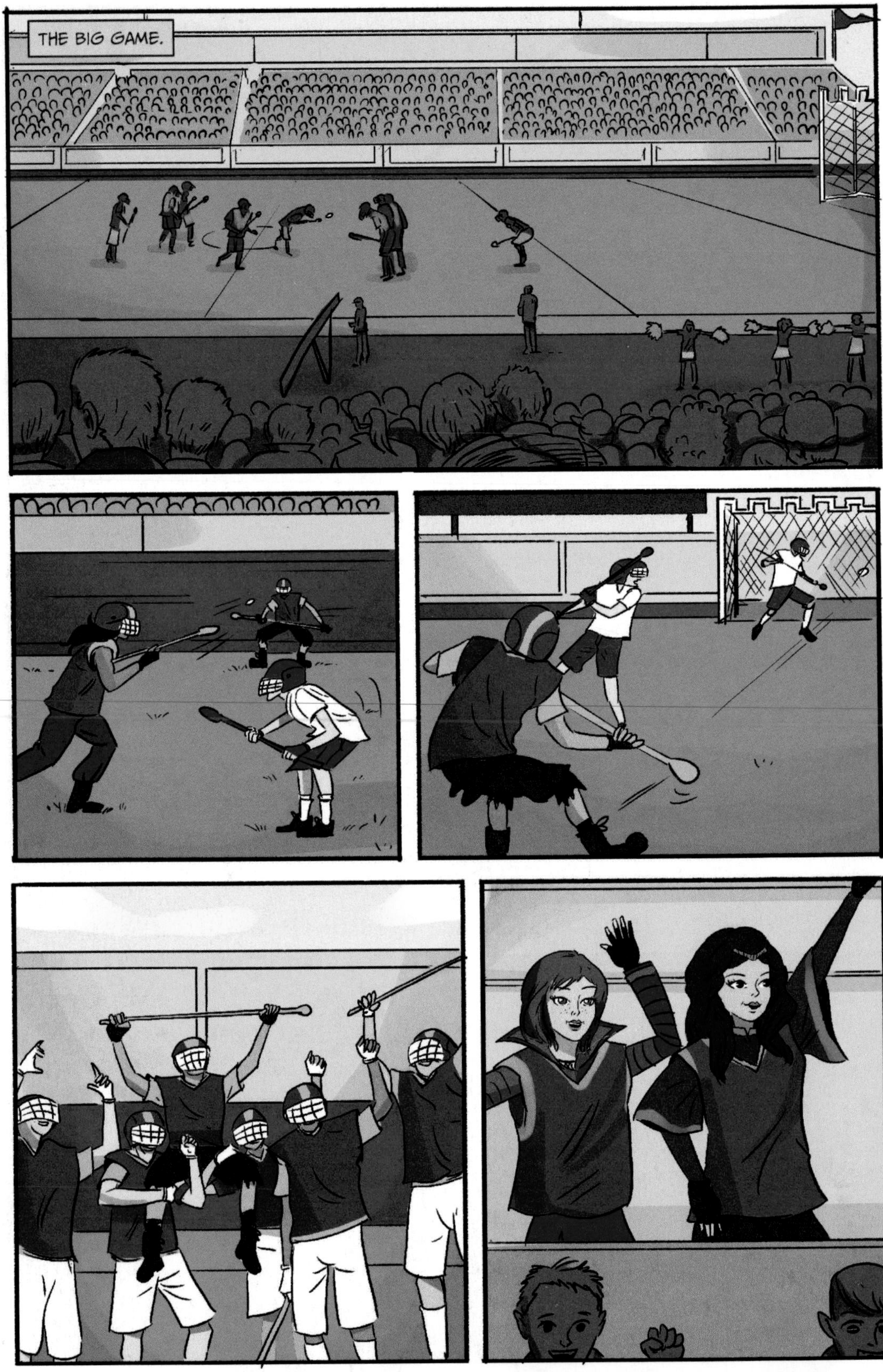
THE BIG GAME.

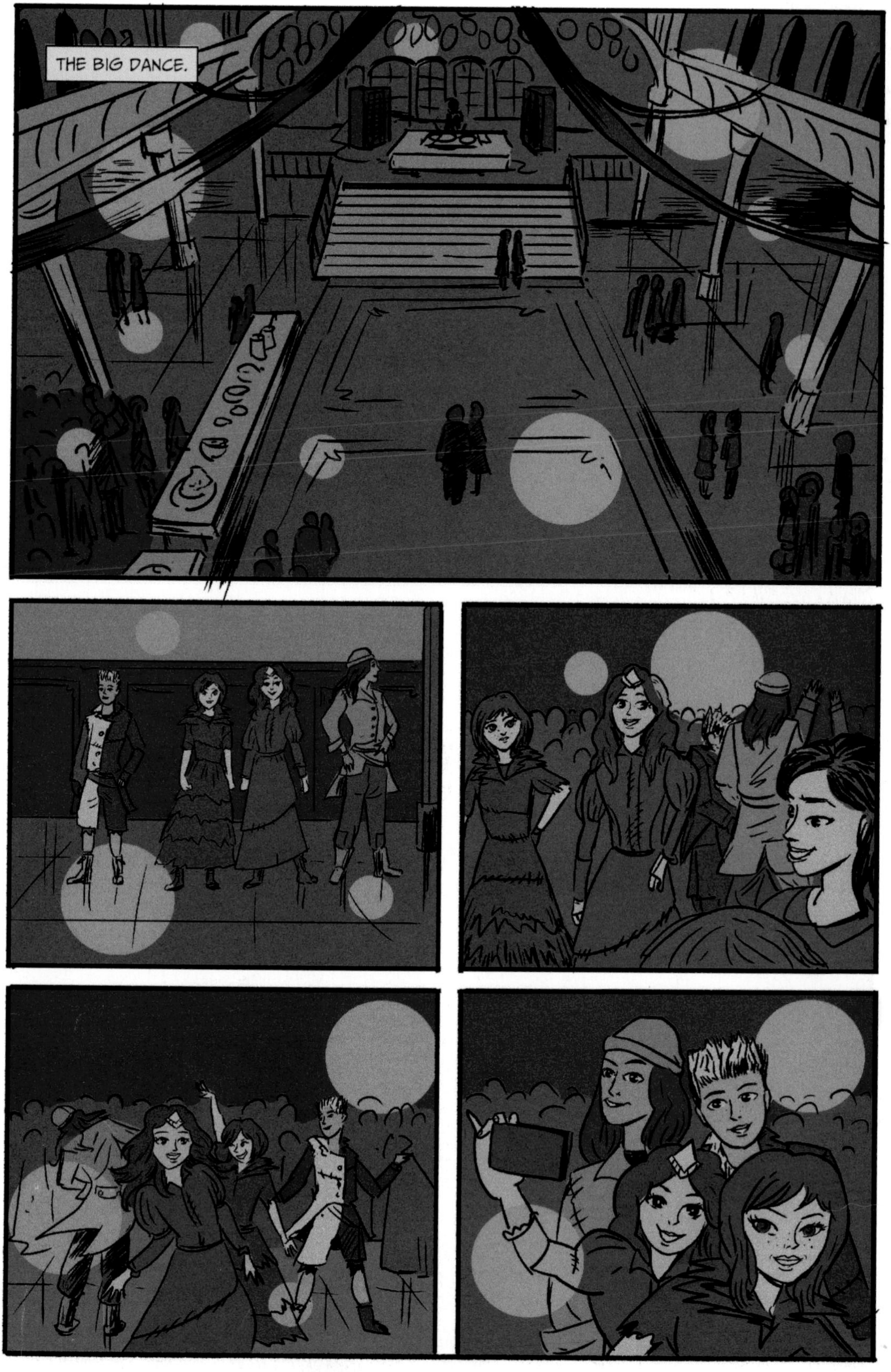
THE BIG DANCE.

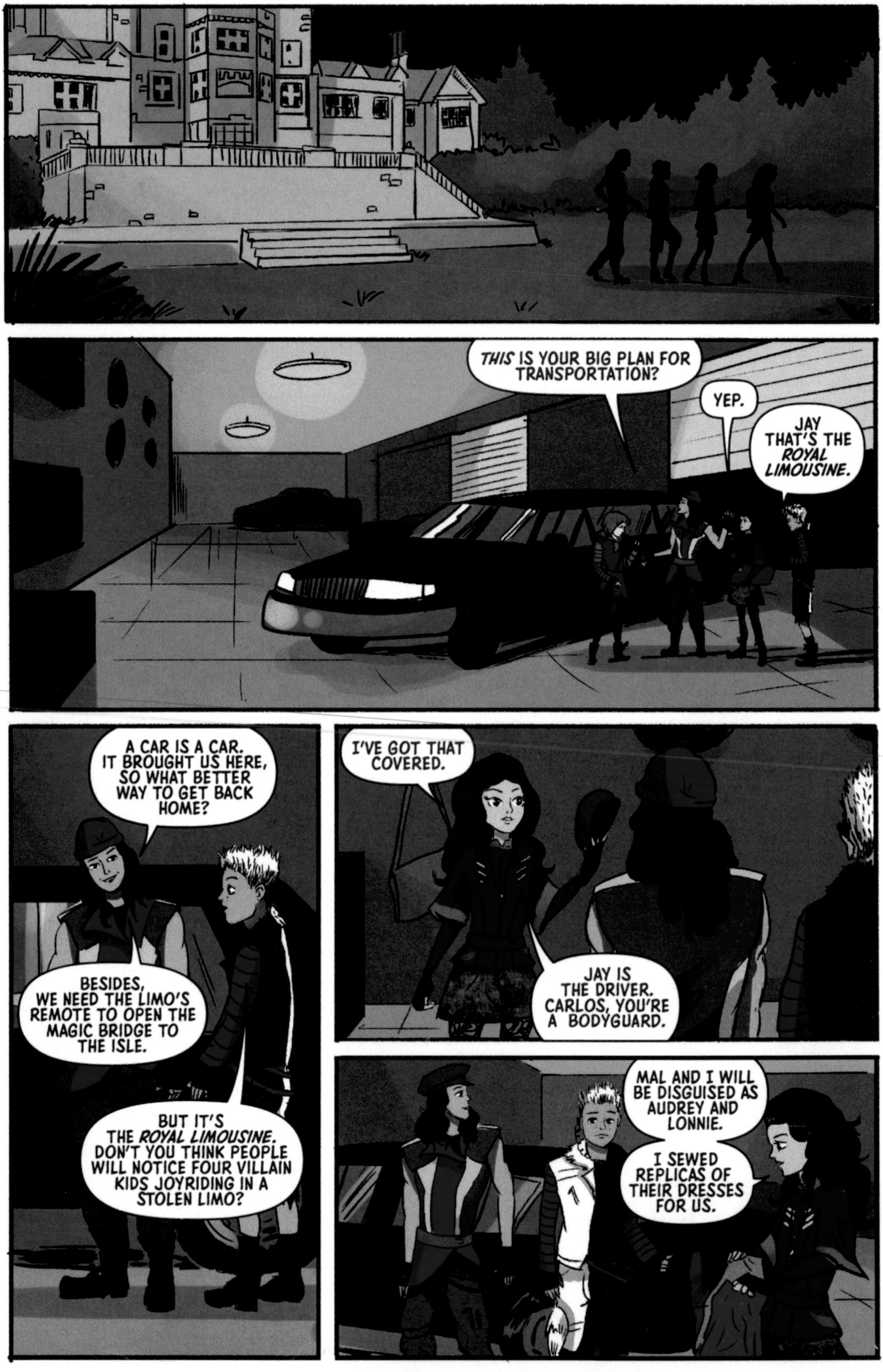
THIS IS YOUR BIG PLAN FOR TRANSPORTATION?
YEP.
JAY THAT'S THE ROYAL LIMOUSINE.
A CAR IS A CAR. IT BROUGHT US HERE, SO WHAT BETTER WAY TO GET BACK HOME?
BESIDES, WE NEED THE LIMO'S REMOTE TO OPEN THE MAGIC BRIDGE TO THE ISLE.
BUT IT'S THE ROYAL LIMOUSINE. DON'T YOU THINK PEOPLE WILL NOTICE FOUR VILLAIN KIDS JOYRIDING IN A STOLEN LIMO?
I'VE GOT THAT COVERED.
JAY IS THE DRIVER. CARLOS, YOU'RE A BODYGUARD.
MAL AND I WILL BE DISGUISED AS AUDREY AND LONNIE.
I SEWED REPLICAS OF THEIR DRESSES FOR US.

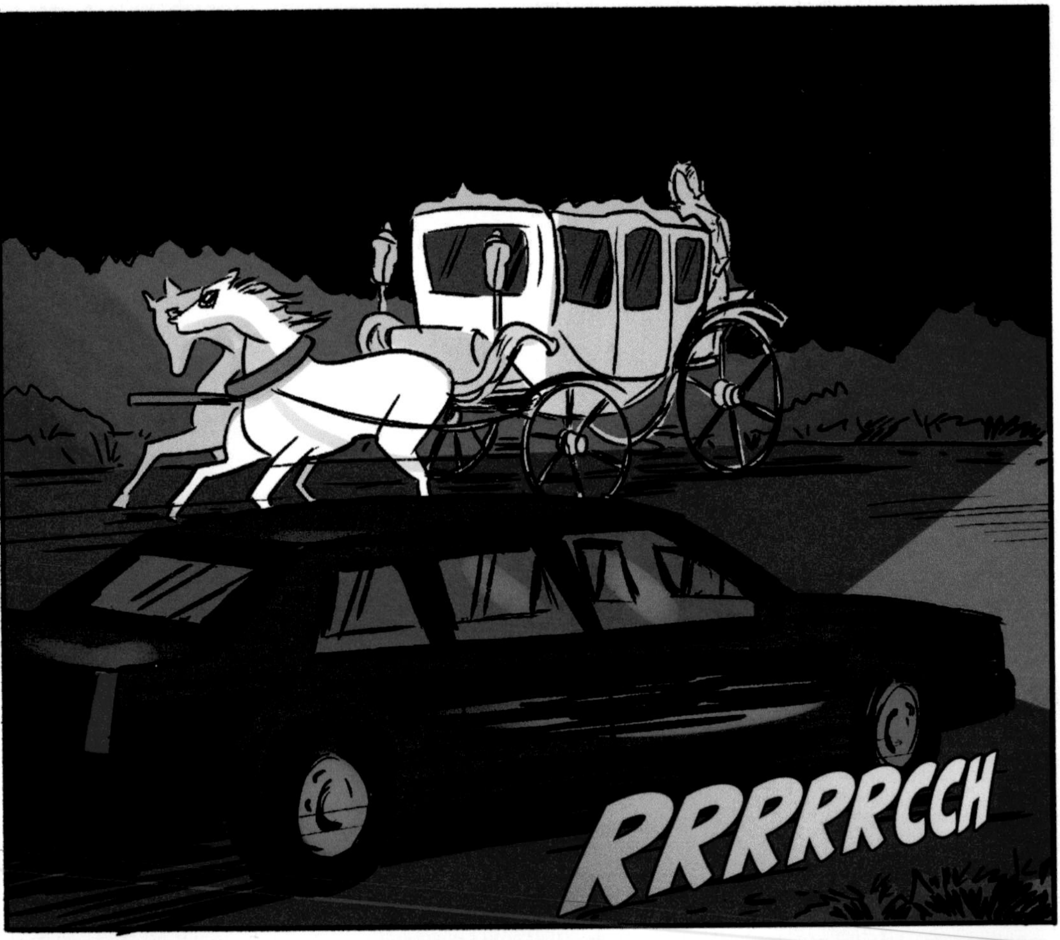
RRRRRCCH

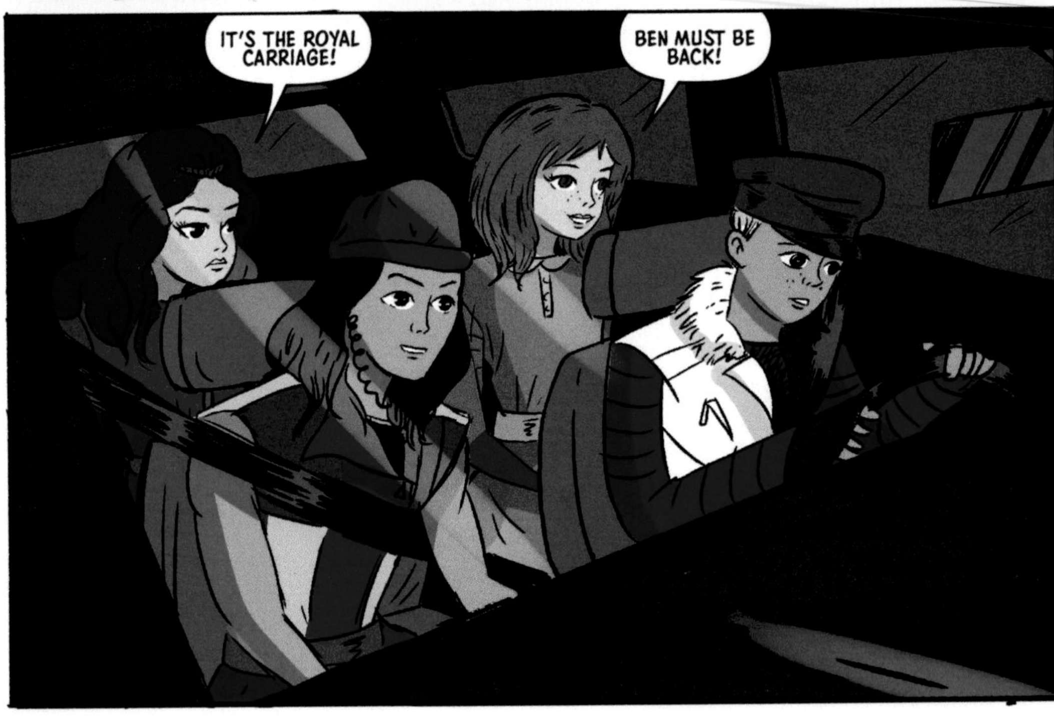
IT'S THE ROYAL CARRIAGE!
BEN MUST BE BACK!

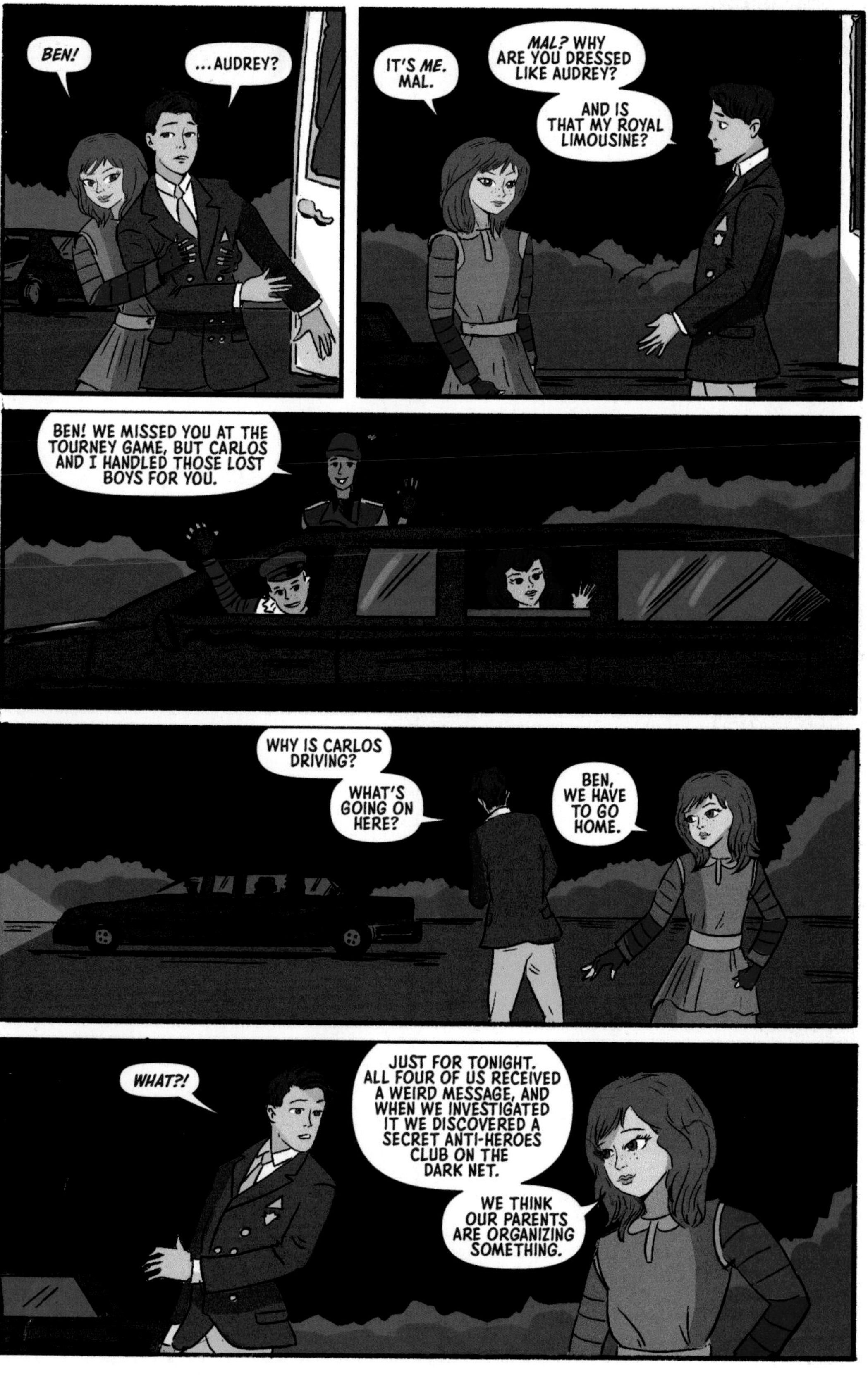
BEN!
...AUDREY?
IT'S *ME.* MAL.
MAL? WHY ARE YOU DRESSED LIKE AUDREY?
AND IS THAT MY ROYAL LIMOUSINE?
BEN! WE MISSED YOU AT THE TOURNEY GAME, BUT CARLOS AND I HANDLED THOSE LOST BOYS FOR YOU.
WHY IS CARLOS DRIVING?
WHAT'S GOING ON HERE?
BEN, WE HAVE TO GO HOME.
WHAT?!
JUST FOR TONIGHT. ALL FOUR OF US RECEIVED A WEIRD MESSAGE, AND WHEN WE INVESTIGATED IT WE DISCOVERED A SECRET ANTI-HEROES CLUB ON THE DARK NET.
WE THINK OUR PARENTS ARE ORGANIZING SOMETHING.

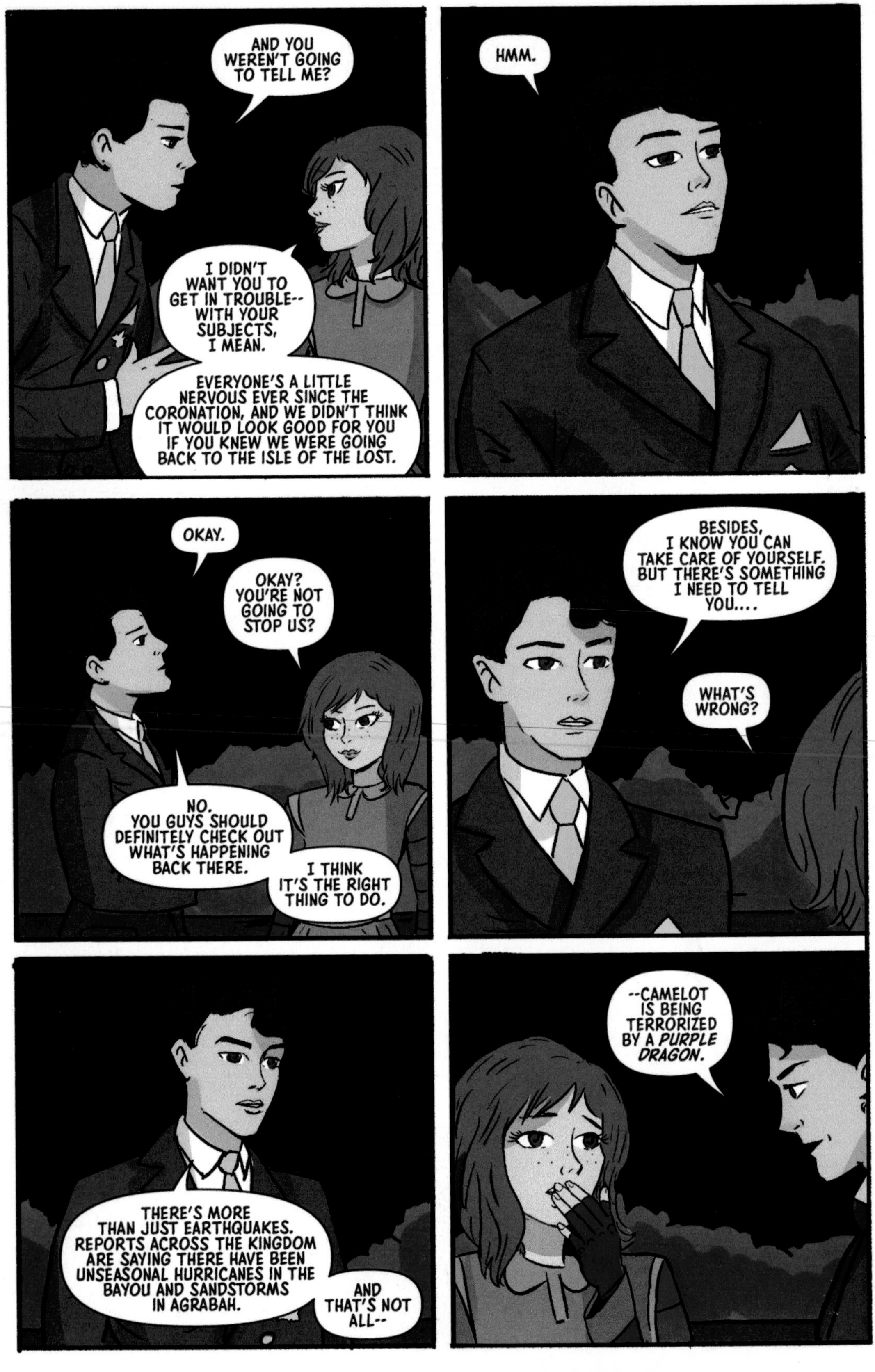
AND YOU WEREN'T GOING TO TELL ME?
I DIDN'T WANT YOU TO GET IN TROUBLE-- WITH YOUR SUBJECTS, I MEAN.
EVERYONE'S A LITTLE NERVOUS EVER SINCE THE CORONATION, AND WE DIDN'T THINK IT WOULD LOOK GOOD FOR YOU IF YOU KNEW WE WERE GOING BACK TO THE ISLE OF THE LOST.
HMM.
OKAY.
OKAY? YOU'RE NOT GOING TO STOP US?
NO. YOU GUYS SHOULD DEFINITELY CHECK OUT WHAT'S HAPPENING BACK THERE.
I THINK IT'S THE RIGHT THING TO DO.
BESIDES, I KNOW YOU CAN TAKE CARE OF YOURSELF. BUT THERE'S SOMETHING I NEED TO TELL YOU....
WHAT'S WRONG?
THERE'S MORE THAN JUST EARTHQUAKES. REPORTS ACROSS THE KINGDOM ARE SAYING THERE HAVE BEEN UNSEASONAL HURRICANES IN THE BAYOU AND SANDSTORMS IN AGRABAH.
AND THAT'S NOT ALL--
--CAMELOT IS BEING TERRORIZED BY A *PURPLE DRAGON*.

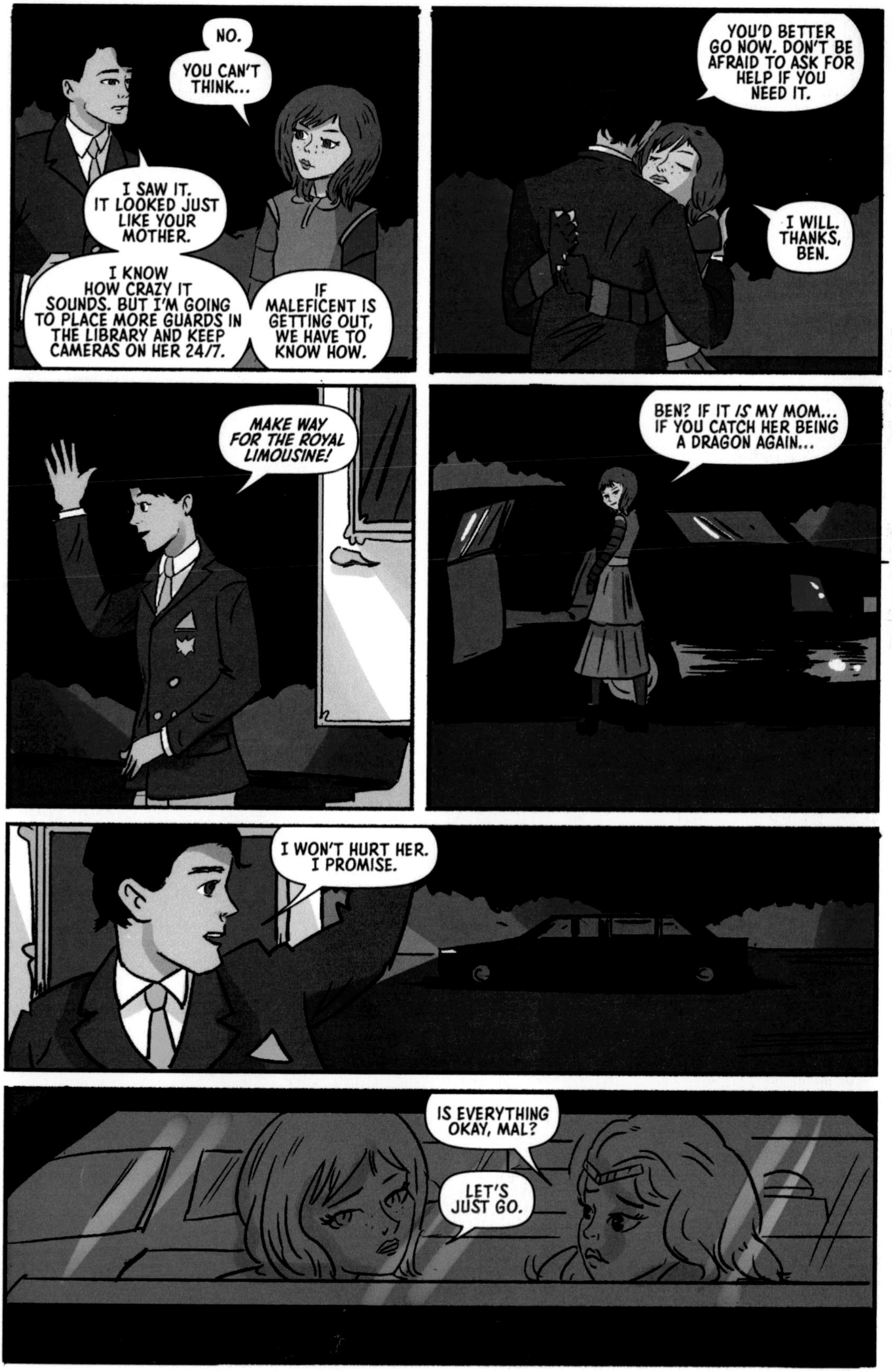
NO.
YOU CAN'T THINK...
I SAW IT. IT LOOKED JUST LIKE YOUR MOTHER.
I KNOW HOW CRAZY IT SOUNDS. BUT I'M GOING TO PLACE MORE GUARDS IN THE LIBRARY AND KEEP CAMERAS ON HER 24/7.
IF MALEFICENT IS GETTING OUT, WE HAVE TO KNOW HOW.
YOU'D BETTER GO NOW. DON'T BE AFRAID TO ASK FOR HELP IF YOU NEED IT.
I WILL. THANKS, BEN.
MAKE WAY FOR THE ROYAL LIMOUSINE!
BEN? IF IT IS MY MOM... IF YOU CATCH HER BEING A DRAGON AGAIN...
I WON'T HURT HER. I PROMISE.
IS EVERYTHING OKAY, MAL?
LET'S JUST GO.

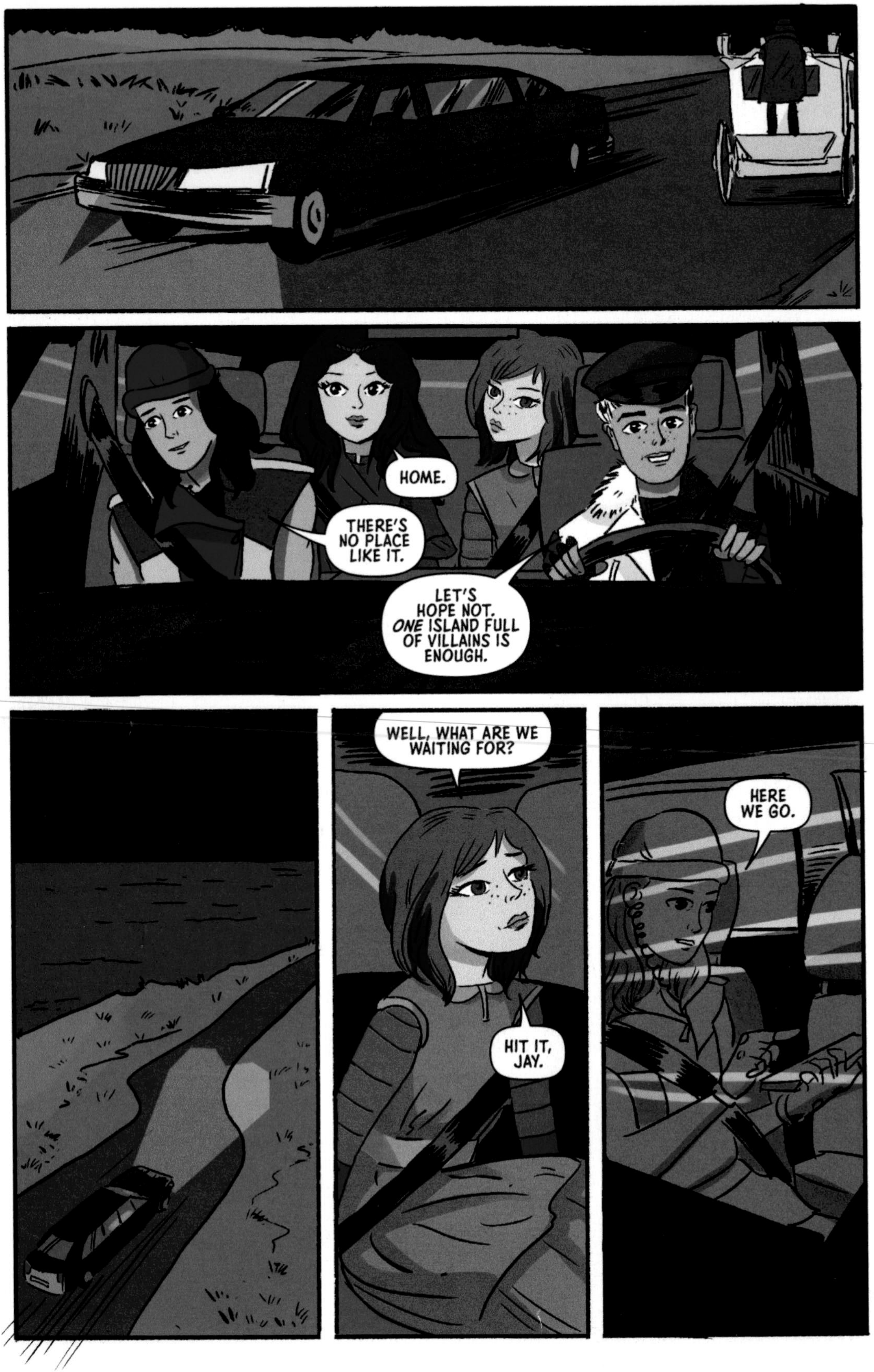
HOME.
THERE'S NO PLACE LIKE IT.
LET'S HOPE NOT. *ONE* ISLAND FULL OF VILLAINS IS ENOUGH.
WELL, WHAT ARE WE WAITING FOR?
HIT IT, JAY.
HERE WE GO.

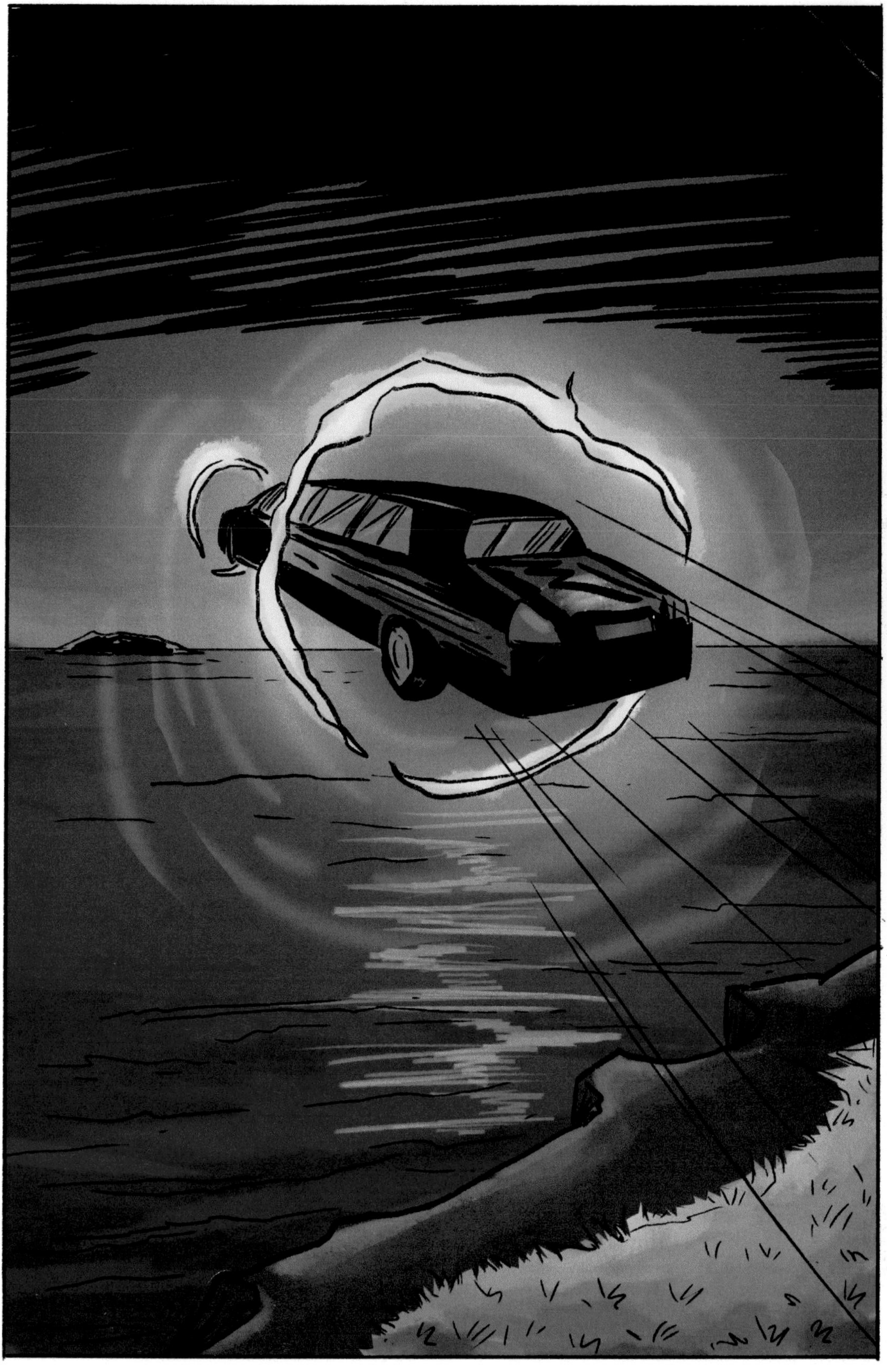

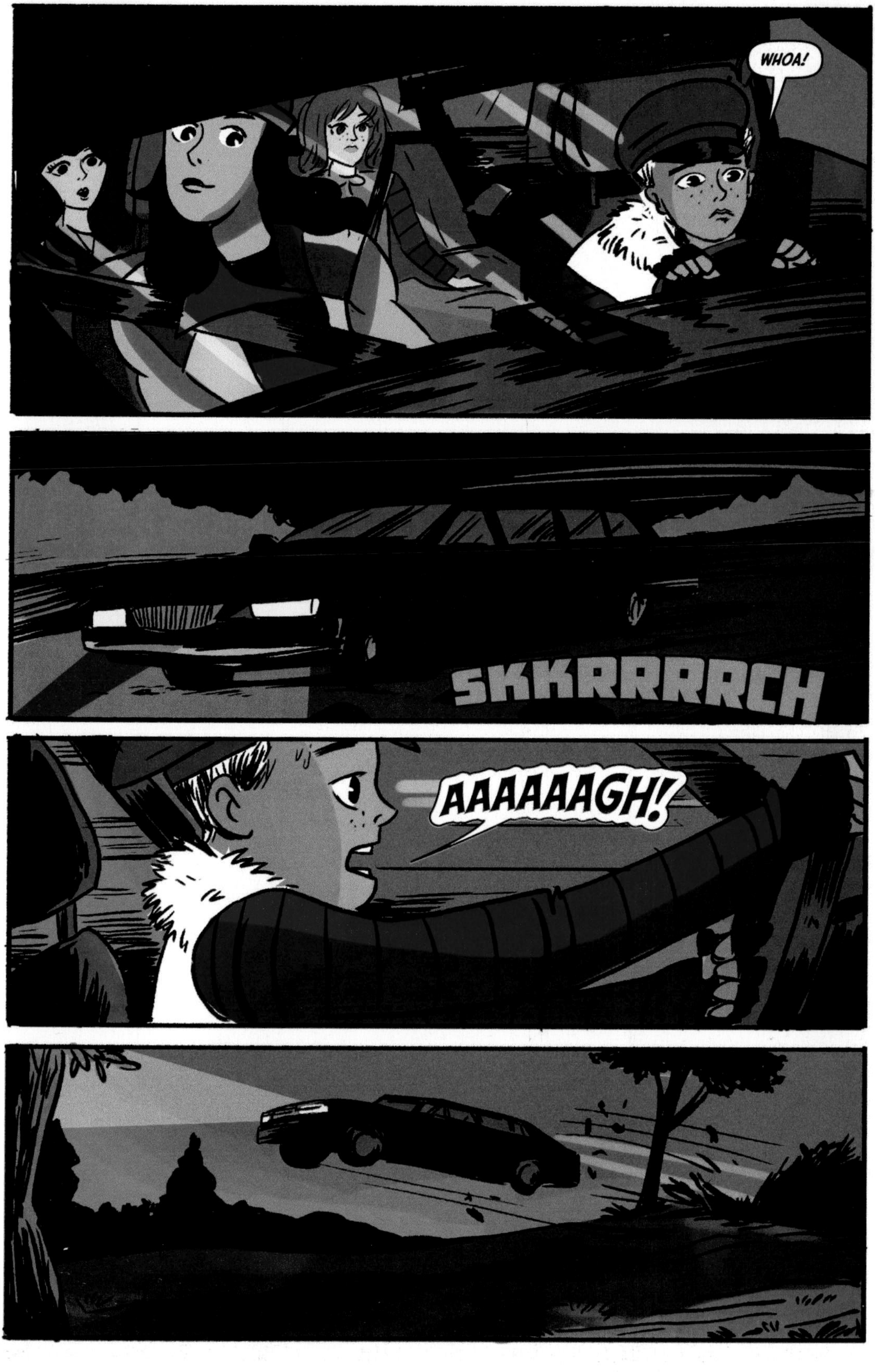
WHOA!
SKKRRRRRCH
AAAAAAGH!

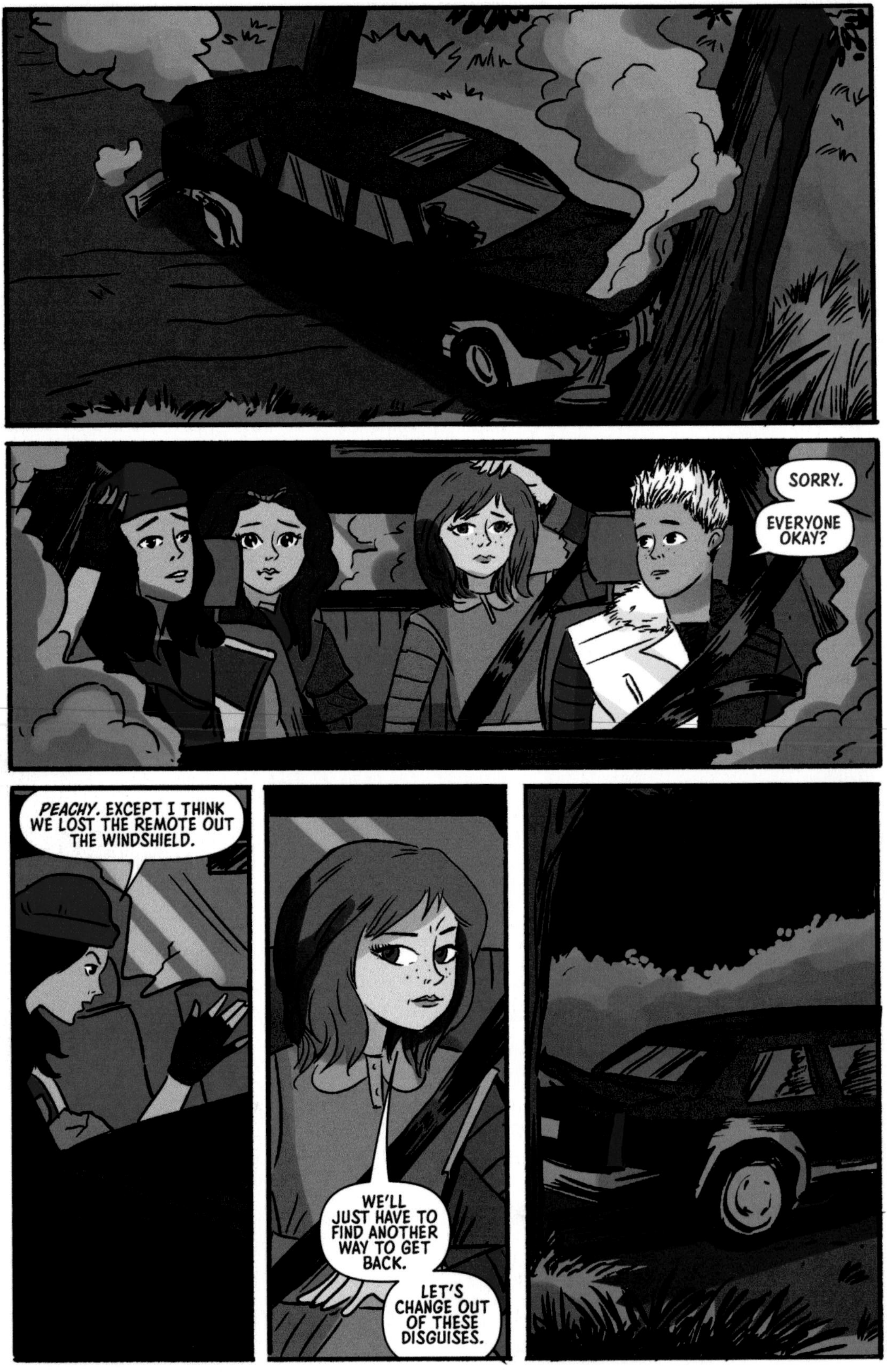
SORRY.
EVERYONE OKAY?
PEACHY. EXCEPT I THINK WE LOST THE REMOTE OUT THE WINDSHIELD.
WE'LL JUST HAVE TO FIND ANOTHER WAY TO GET BACK.
LET'S CHANGE OUT OF THESE DISGUISES.

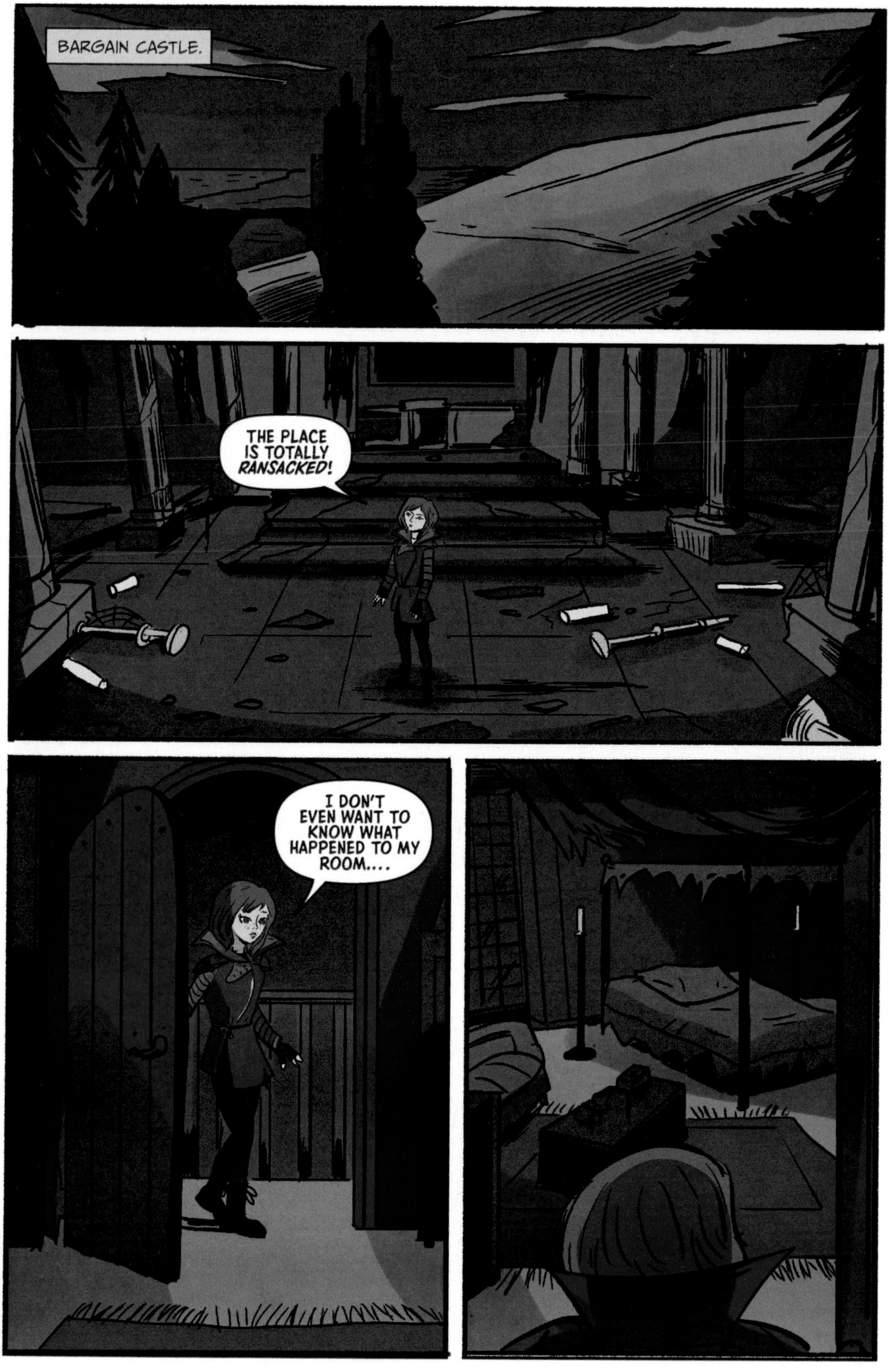
BARGAIN CASTLE.
THE PLACE IS TOTALLY *RANSACKED!*
I DON'T EVEN WANT TO KNOW WHAT HAPPENED TO MY ROOM....

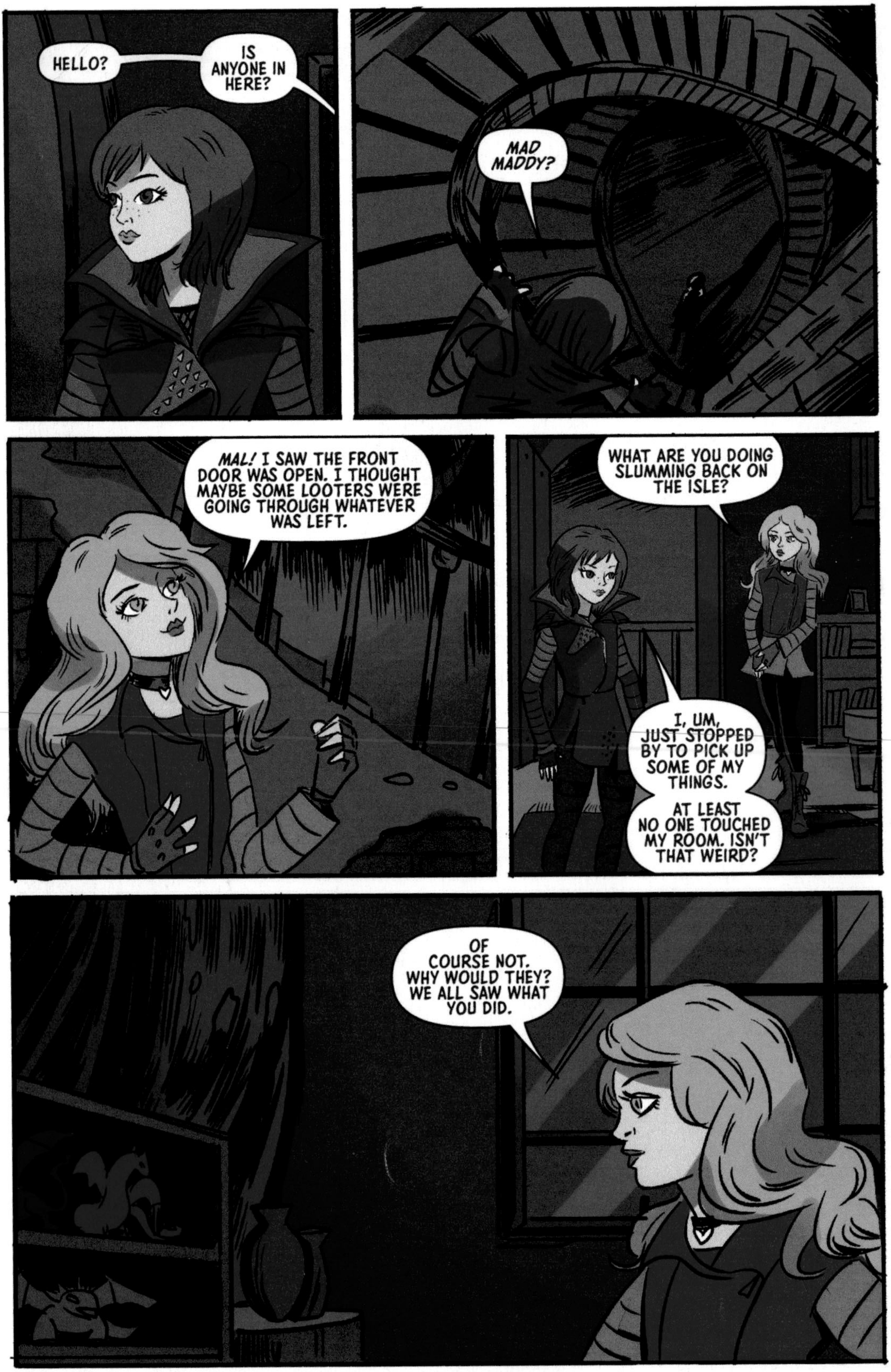
HELLO?
IS ANYONE IN HERE?
MAD MADDY?
MAL! I SAW THE FRONT DOOR WAS OPEN. I THOUGHT MAYBE SOME LOOTERS WERE GOING THROUGH WHATEVER WAS LEFT.
WHAT ARE YOU DOING SLUMMING BACK ON THE ISLE?
I, UM, JUST STOPPED BY TO PICK UP SOME OF MY THINGS.
AT LEAST NO ONE TOUCHED MY ROOM. ISN'T THAT WEIRD?
OF COURSE NOT. WHY WOULD THEY? WE ALL SAW WHAT YOU DID.

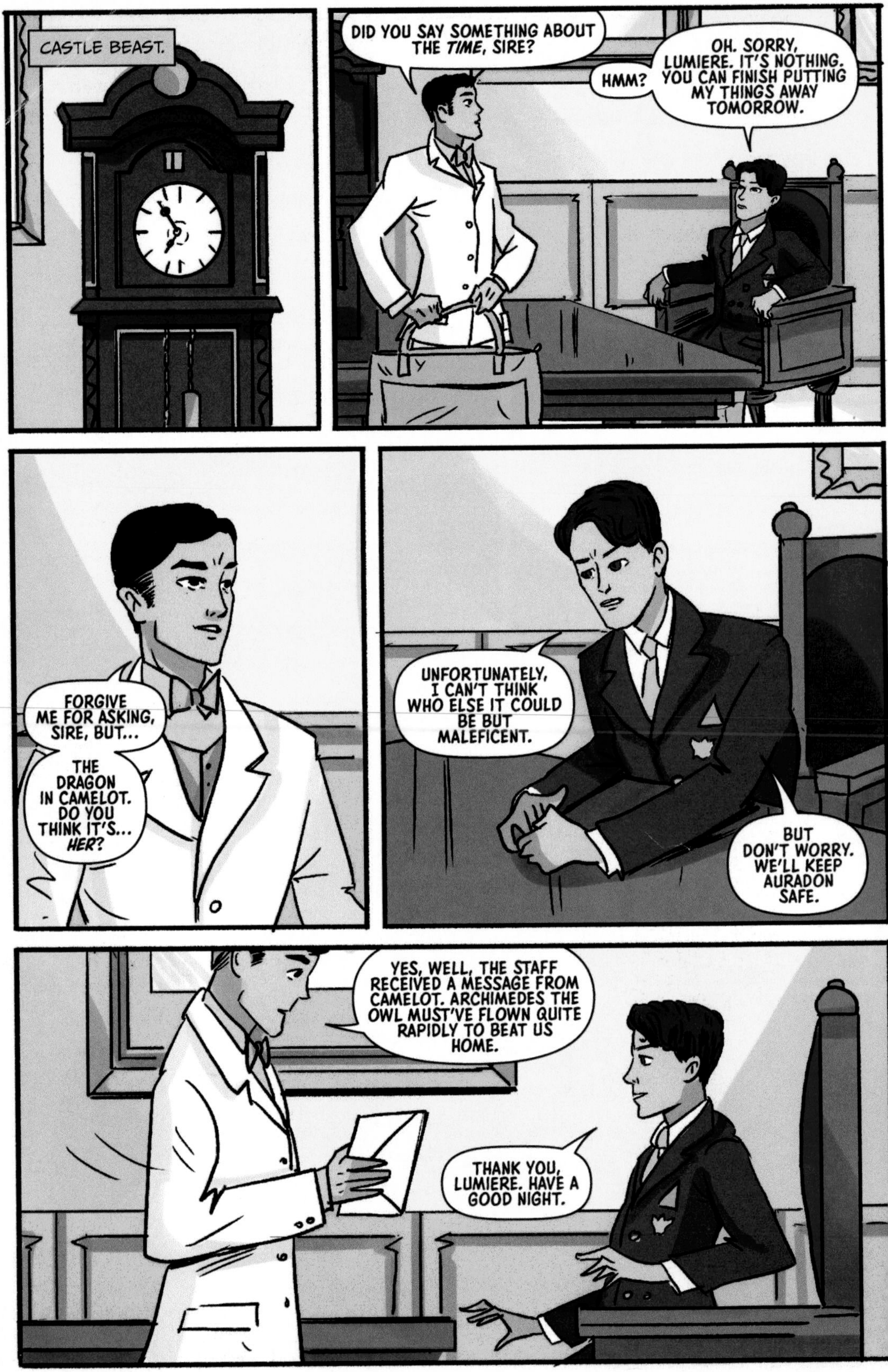
CASTLE BEAST.
DID YOU SAY SOMETHING ABOUT THE *TIME*, SIRE?
HMM?
OH. SORRY, LUMIERE. IT'S NOTHING. YOU CAN FINISH PUTTING MY THINGS AWAY TOMORROW.
FORGIVE ME FOR ASKING, SIRE, BUT...
THE DRAGON IN CAMELOT. DO YOU THINK IT'S... *HER*?
UNFORTUNATELY, I CAN'T THINK WHO ELSE IT COULD BE BUT MALEFICENT.
BUT DON'T WORRY. WE'LL KEEP AURADON SAFE.
YES, WELL, THE STAFF RECEIVED A MESSAGE FROM CAMELOT. ARCHIMEDES THE OWL MUST'VE FLOWN QUITE RAPIDLY TO BEAT US HOME.
THANK YOU, LUMIERE. HAVE A GOOD NIGHT.

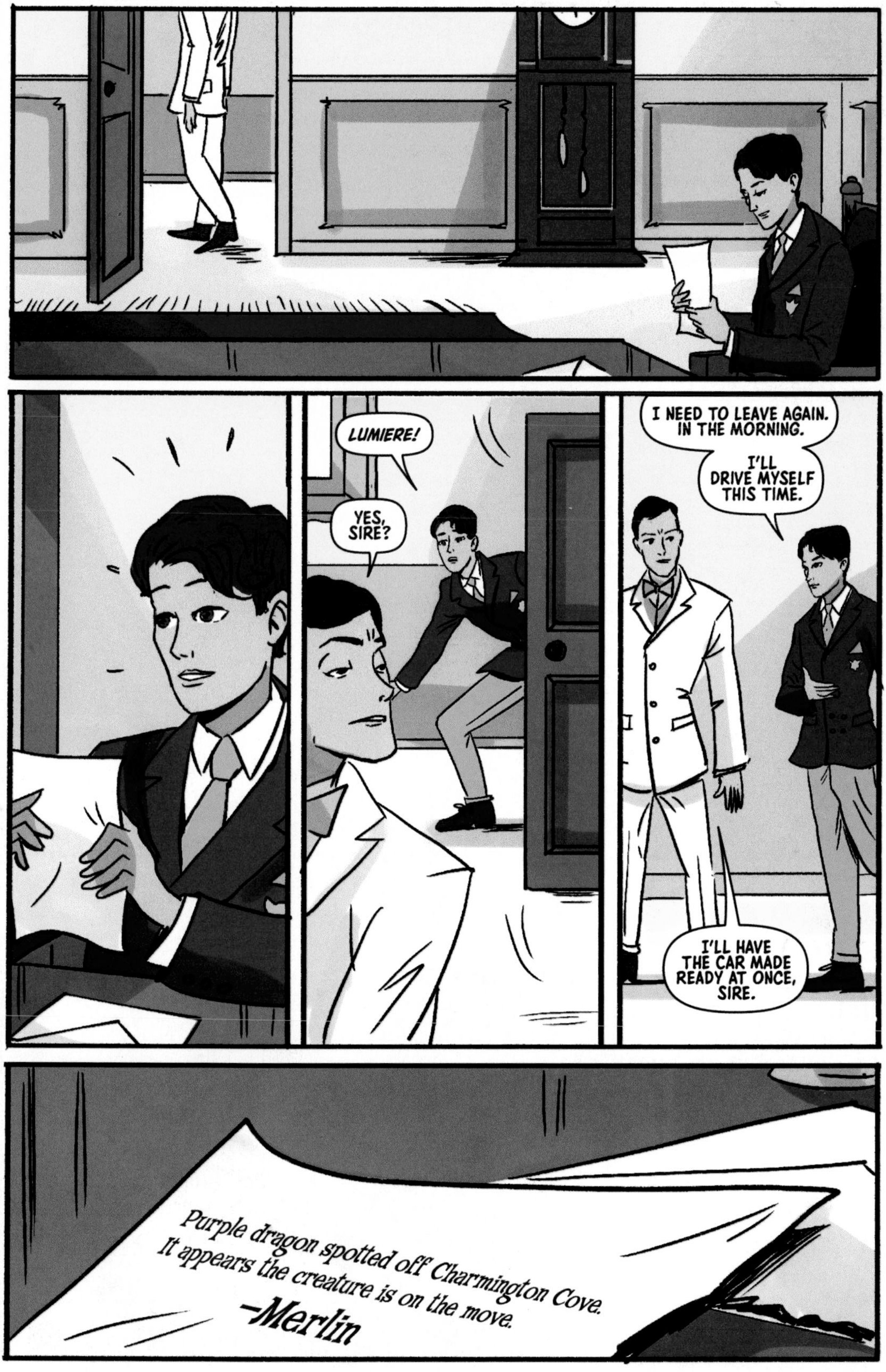
LUMIERE!
YES, SIRE?
I NEED TO LEAVE AGAIN. IN THE MORNING.
I'LL DRIVE MYSELF THIS TIME.
I'LL HAVE THE CAR MADE READY AT ONCE, SIRE.
Purple dragon spotted off Charmington Cove.
It appears the creature is on the move.
–Merlin

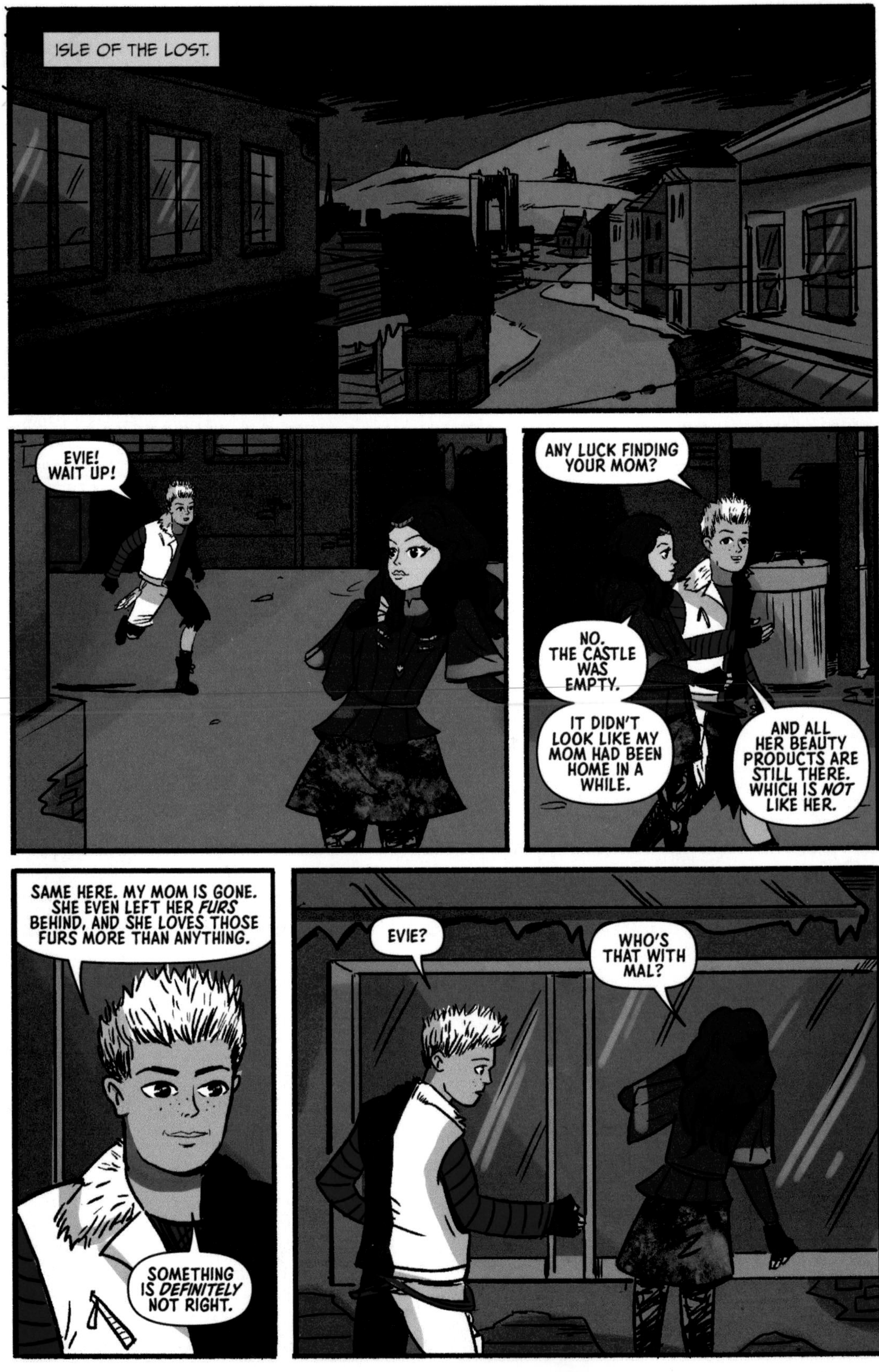
ISLE OF THE LOST.
EVIE! WAIT UP!
ANY LUCK FINDING YOUR MOM?
NO. THE CASTLE WAS EMPTY.
IT DIDN'T LOOK LIKE MY MOM HAD BEEN HOME IN A WHILE.
AND ALL HER BEAUTY PRODUCTS ARE STILL THERE. WHICH IS *NOT* LIKE HER.
SAME HERE. MY MOM IS GONE. *SHE* EVEN LEFT HER *FURS* BEHIND, AND SHE LOVES THOSE FURS MORE THAN ANYTHING.
SOMETHING IS *DEFINITELY* NOT RIGHT.
EVIE?
WHO'S THAT WITH MAL?

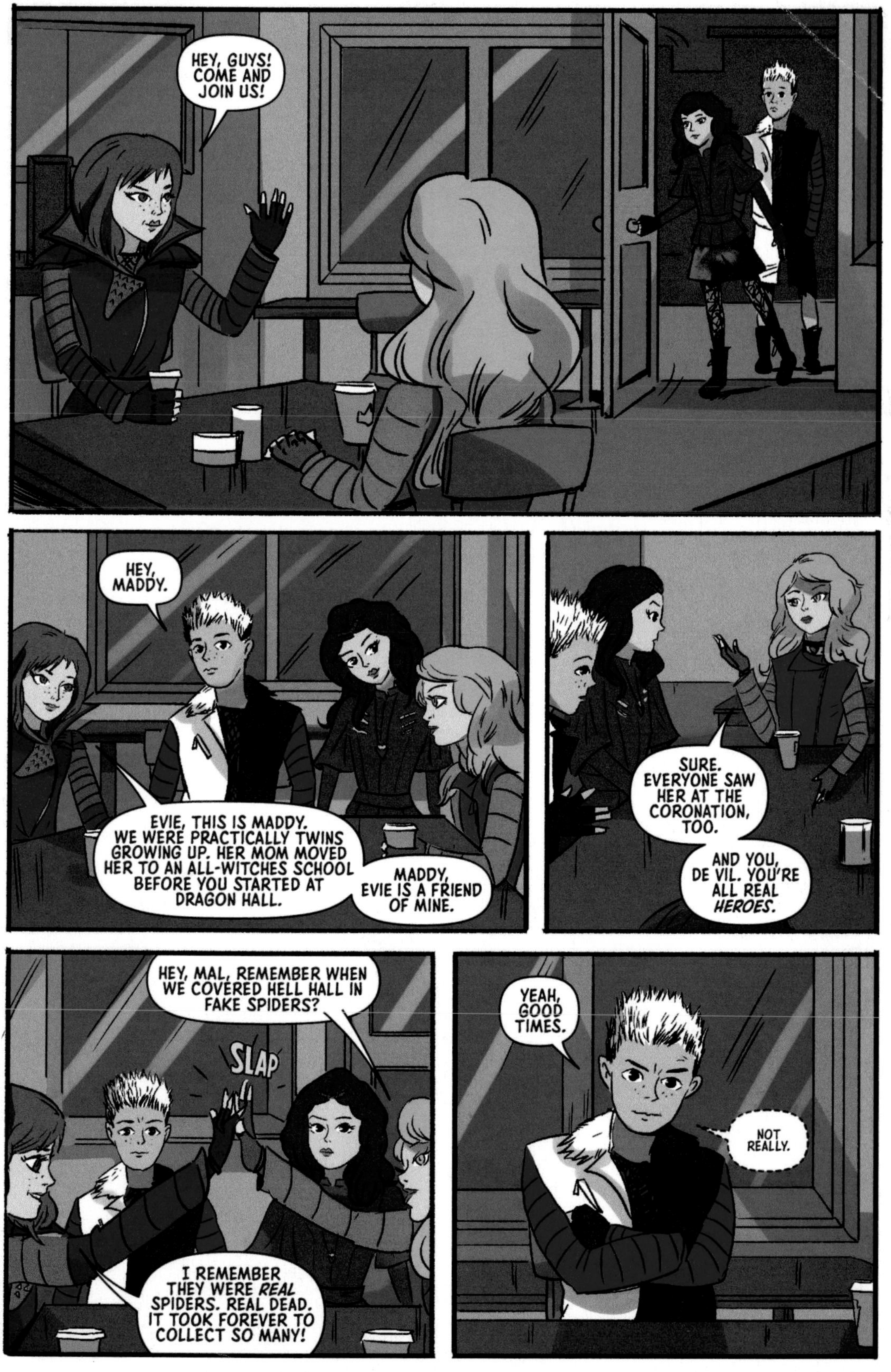
HEY, GUYS! COME AND JOIN US!
HEY, MADDY.
EVIE, THIS IS MADDY. WE WERE PRACTICALLY TWINS GROWING UP. HER MOM MOVED HER TO AN ALL-WITCHES SCHOOL BEFORE YOU STARTED AT DRAGON HALL.
MADDY, EVIE IS A FRIEND OF MINE.
SURE. EVERYONE SAW HER AT THE CORONATION, TOO.
AND YOU, DE VIL. YOU'RE ALL REAL *HEROES*.
HEY, MAL, REMEMBER WHEN WE COVERED HELL HALL IN FAKE SPIDERS?
SLAP
I REMEMBER THEY WERE *REAL* SPIDERS. REAL DEAD. IT TOOK FOREVER TO COLLECT SO MANY!
YEAH, GOOD TIMES.
NOT REALLY.

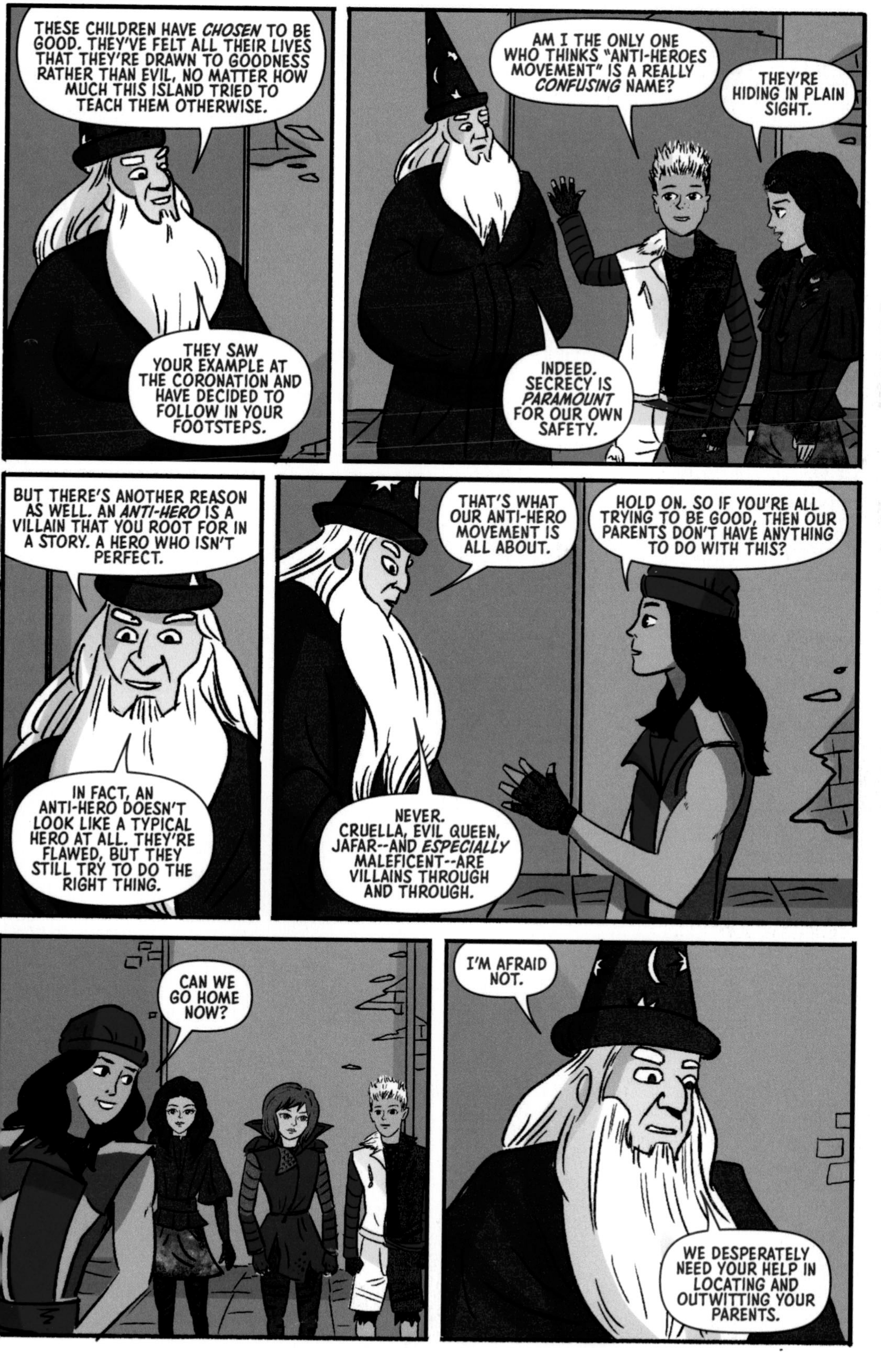
THESE CHILDREN HAVE *CHOSEN* TO BE GOOD. THEY'VE FELT ALL THEIR LIVES THAT THEY'RE DRAWN TO GOODNESS RATHER THAN EVIL, NO MATTER HOW MUCH THIS ISLAND TRIED TO TEACH THEM OTHERWISE.
THEY SAW YOUR EXAMPLE AT THE CORONATION AND HAVE DECIDED TO FOLLOW IN YOUR FOOTSTEPS.
AM I THE ONLY ONE WHO THINKS "ANTI-HEROES MOVEMENT" IS A REALLY *CONFUSING* NAME?
THEY'RE HIDING IN PLAIN SIGHT.
INDEED. SECRECY IS *PARAMOUNT* FOR OUR OWN SAFETY.
BUT THERE'S ANOTHER REASON AS WELL. AN *ANTI-HERO* IS A VILLAIN THAT YOU ROOT FOR IN A STORY. A HERO WHO ISN'T PERFECT.
IN FACT, AN ANTI-HERO DOESN'T LOOK LIKE A TYPICAL HERO AT ALL. THEY'RE FLAWED, BUT THEY STILL TRY TO DO THE RIGHT THING.
THAT'S WHAT OUR ANTI-HERO MOVEMENT IS ALL ABOUT.
HOLD ON. SO IF YOU'RE ALL TRYING TO BE GOOD, THEN OUR PARENTS DON'T HAVE ANYTHING TO DO WITH THIS?
NEVER. CRUELLA, EVIL QUEEN, JAFAR--AND *ESPECIALLY* MALEFICENT--ARE VILLAINS THROUGH AND THROUGH.
CAN WE GO HOME NOW?
I'M AFRAID NOT.
WE DESPERATELY NEED YOUR HELP IN LOCATING AND OUTWITTING YOUR PARENTS.

YOU DON'T KNOW WHERE THEY ARE?

THEY DISAPPEARED IN THE CHAOS THAT ENSUED WHEN MALEFICENT BROKE OPEN THE DOME.

NOW I HAVE A QUESTION FOR YOU: HAVE YOU BEEN EXPERIENCING ANY *EARTHQUAKES* IN AURADON? TREMORS, VIBRATIONS, AND ONCE IN A WHILE, A REAL RUMBLE?

WE HAVE. NOT JUST EARTHQUAKES, THOUGH. BEN SAYS THE WHOLE KINGDOM IS SUFFERING FROM WEIRD UNSEASONAL WEATHER.

BUT WHAT DOES THAT HAVE TO DO WITH OUR MISSING PARENTS?

IT'S WORSE THAN I FEARED.

I THINK IT'S TIME FOR ME TO TELL YOU A LITTLE BIT ABOUT THE HISTORY OF THIS ISLAND.

AS YOU KNOW, WHEN ALL THE VILLAINS WERE PLACED ON THE ISLE OF THE LOST, FAIRY GODMOTHER CREATED THE DOME TO KEEP MAGIC OUT OF THEIR HANDS, SO THEY WOULD NEVER THREATEN AURADON'S PEACE AGAIN.

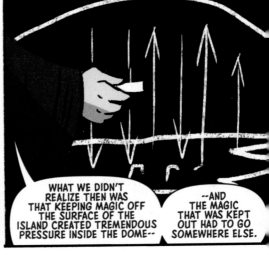

WHAT WE DIDN'T REALIZE THEN WAS THAT KEEPING MAGIC OFF THE SURFACE OF THE ISLAND CREATED TREMENDOUS PRESSURE INSIDE THE DOME--

--AND THE MAGIC THAT WAS KEPT OUT HAD TO GO SOMEWHERE ELSE.

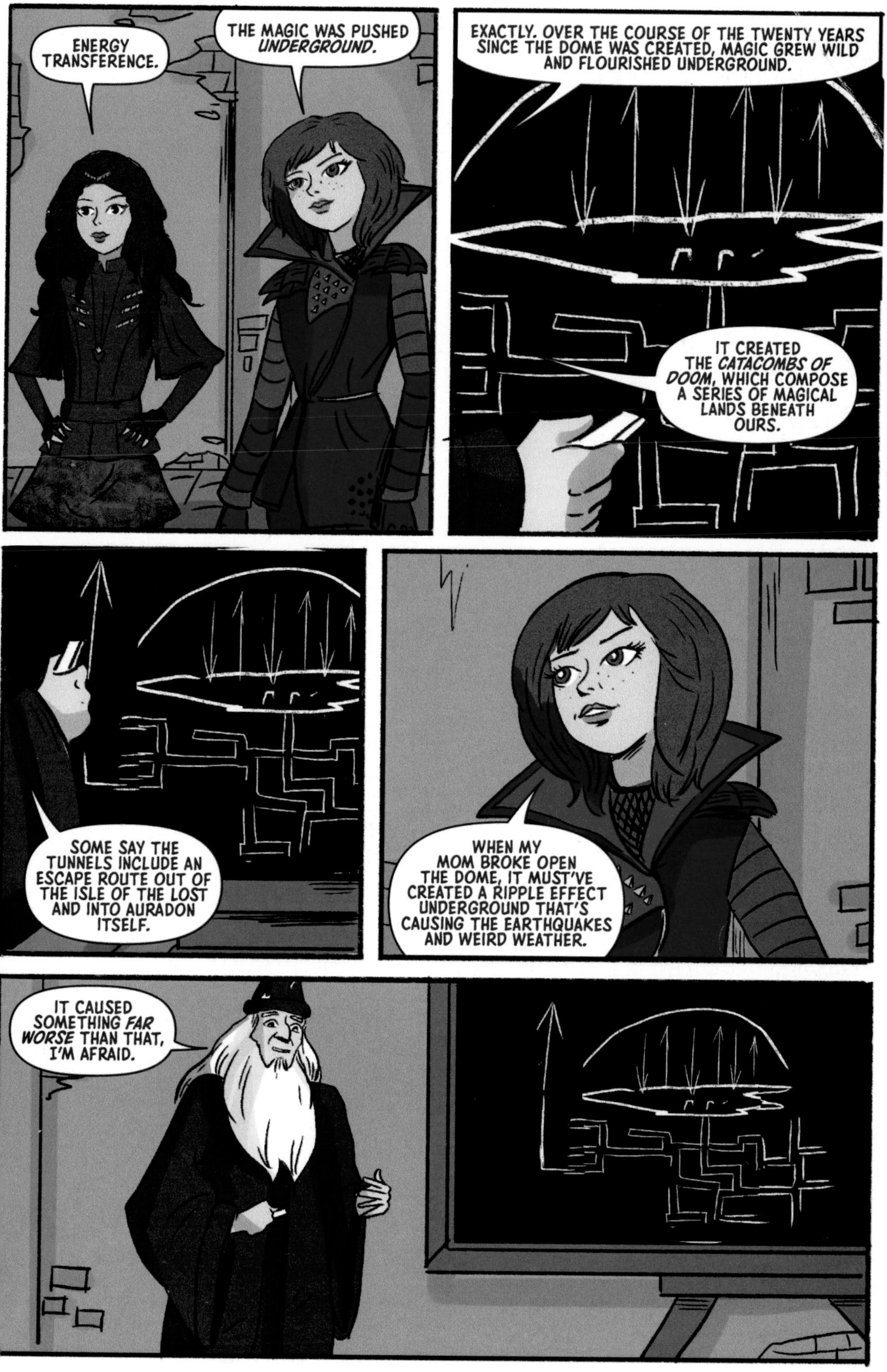
ENERGY TRANSFERENCE.
THE MAGIC WAS PUSHED *UNDERGROUND.*
EXACTLY. OVER THE COURSE OF THE TWENTY YEARS SINCE THE DOME WAS CREATED, MAGIC GREW WILD AND FLOURISHED UNDERGROUND.
IT CREATED THE *CATACOMBS OF DOOM*, WHICH COMPOSE A SERIES OF MAGICAL LANDS BENEATH OURS.
SOME SAY THE TUNNELS INCLUDE AN ESCAPE ROUTE OUT OF THE ISLE OF THE LOST AND INTO AURADON ITSELF.
WHEN MY MOM BROKE OPEN THE DOME, IT MUST'VE CREATED A RIPPLE EFFECT UNDERGROUND THAT'S CAUSING THE EARTHQUAKES AND WEIRD WEATHER.
IT CAUSED SOMETHING *FAR WORSE* THAN THAT, I'M AFRAID.

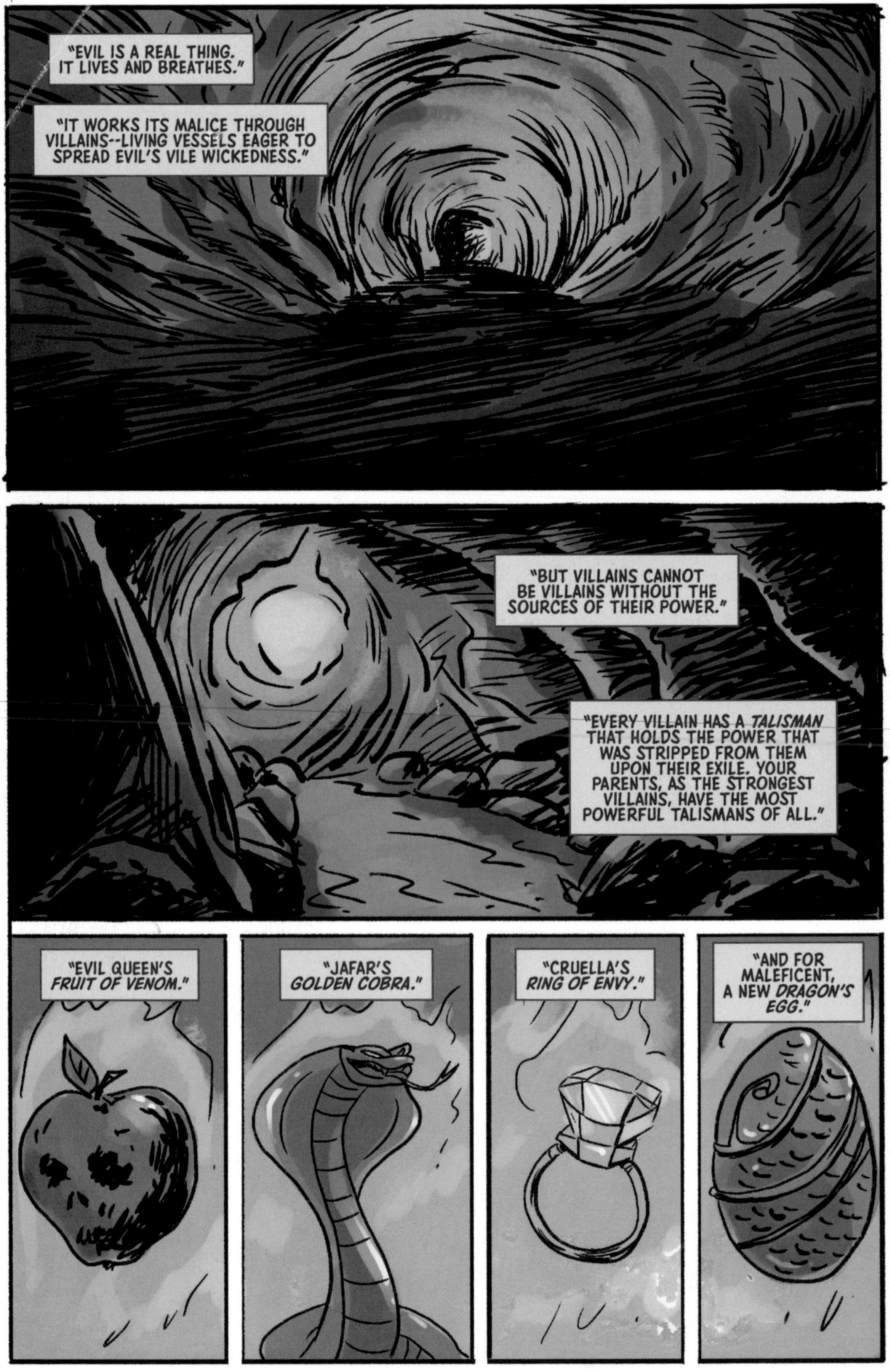
"EVIL IS A REAL THING. IT LIVES AND BREATHES."
"IT WORKS ITS MALICE THROUGH VILLAINS--LIVING VESSELS EAGER TO SPREAD EVIL'S VILE WICKEDNESS."
"BUT VILLAINS CANNOT BE VILLAINS WITHOUT THE SOURCES OF THEIR POWER."
"EVERY VILLAIN HAS A *TALISMAN* THAT HOLDS THE POWER THAT WAS STRIPPED FROM THEM UPON THEIR EXILE. YOUR PARENTS, AS THE STRONGEST VILLAINS, HAVE THE MOST POWERFUL TALISMANS OF ALL."
"EVIL QUEEN'S *FRUIT OF VENOM.*"
"JAFAR'S *GOLDEN COBRA.*"
"CRUELLA'S *RING OF ENVY.*"
"AND FOR MALEFICENT, A NEW *DRAGON'S EGG.*"

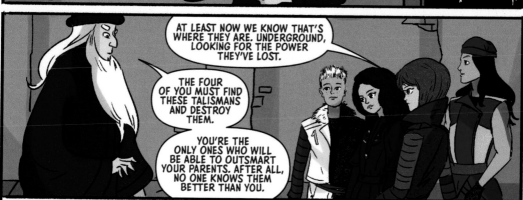

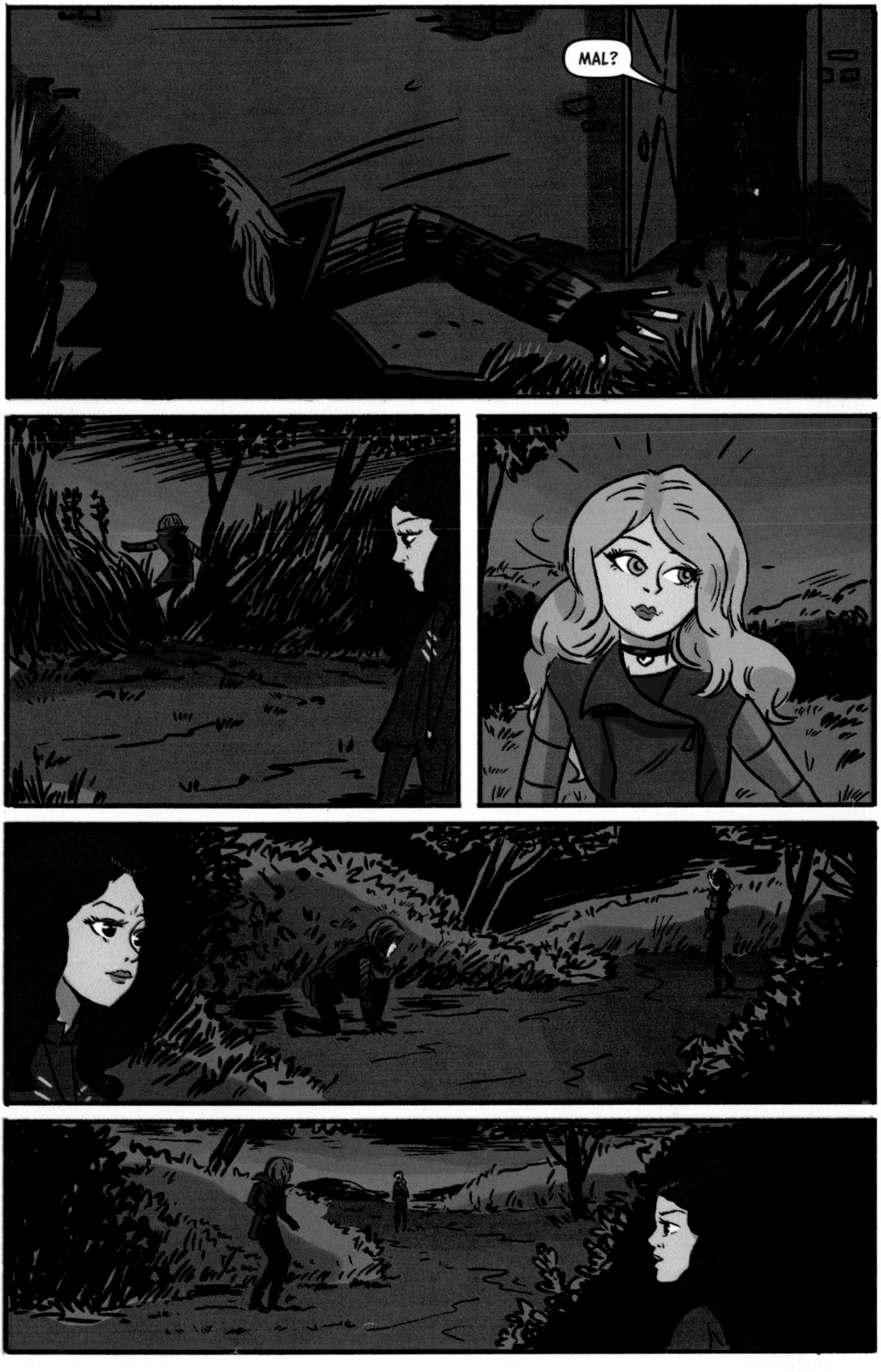
MAL?

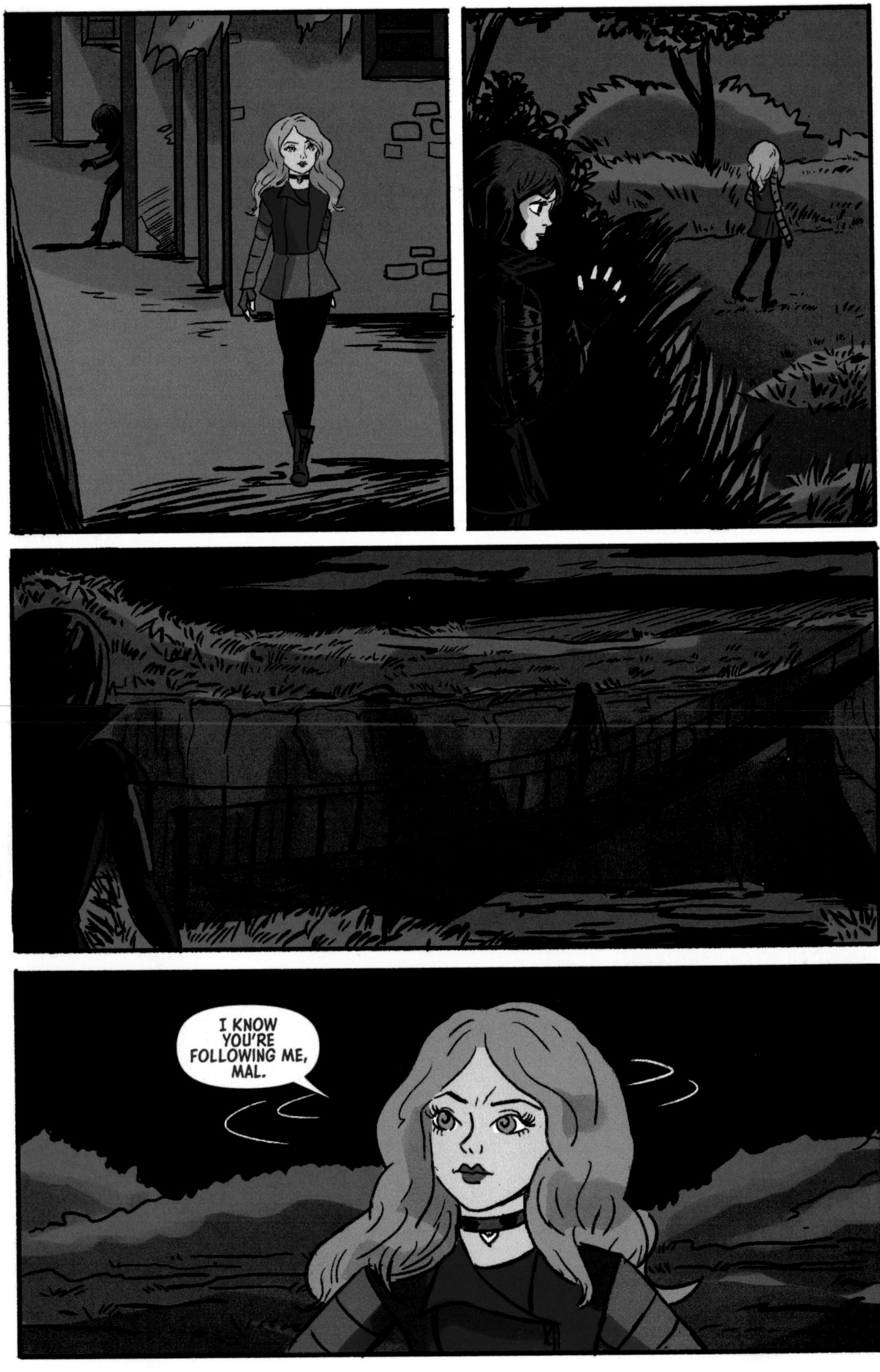
I KNOW YOU'RE FOLLOWING ME, MAL.

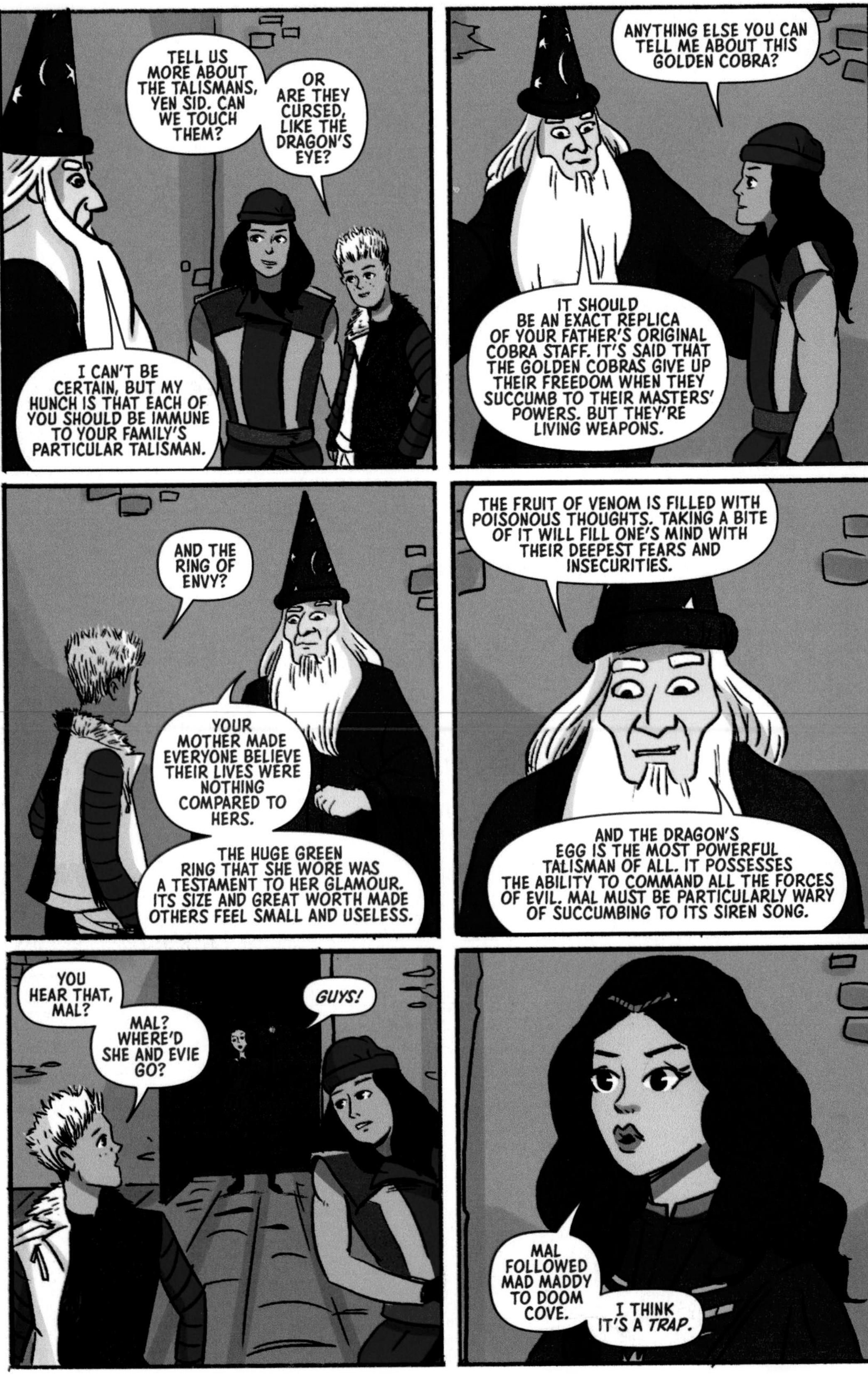
TELL US MORE ABOUT THE TALISMANS, YEN SID. CAN WE TOUCH THEM?
OR ARE THEY CURSED, LIKE THE DRAGON'S EYE?
I CAN'T BE CERTAIN, BUT MY HUNCH IS THAT EACH OF YOU SHOULD BE IMMUNE TO YOUR FAMILY'S PARTICULAR TALISMAN.
ANYTHING ELSE YOU CAN TELL ME ABOUT THIS GOLDEN COBRA?
IT SHOULD BE AN EXACT REPLICA OF YOUR FATHER'S ORIGINAL COBRA STAFF. IT'S SAID THAT THE GOLDEN COBRAS GIVE UP THEIR FREEDOM WHEN THEY SUCCUMB TO THEIR MASTERS' POWERS. BUT THEY'RE LIVING WEAPONS.
AND THE RING OF ENVY?
YOUR MOTHER MADE EVERYONE BELIEVE THEIR LIVES WERE NOTHING COMPARED TO HERS.
THE HUGE GREEN RING THAT SHE WORE WAS A TESTAMENT TO HER GLAMOUR. ITS SIZE AND GREAT WORTH MADE OTHERS FEEL SMALL AND USELESS.
THE FRUIT OF VENOM IS FILLED WITH POISONOUS THOUGHTS. TAKING A BITE OF IT WILL FILL ONE'S MIND WITH THEIR DEEPEST FEARS AND INSECURITIES.
AND THE DRAGON'S EGG IS THE MOST POWERFUL TALISMAN OF ALL. IT POSSESSES THE ABILITY TO COMMAND ALL THE FORCES OF EVIL. MAL MUST BE PARTICULARLY WARY OF SUCCUMBING TO ITS SIREN SONG.
YOU HEAR THAT, MAL?
MAL? WHERE'D SHE AND EVIE GO?
GUYS!
MAL FOLLOWED MAD MADDY TO DOOM COVE.
I THINK IT'S A *TRAP*.

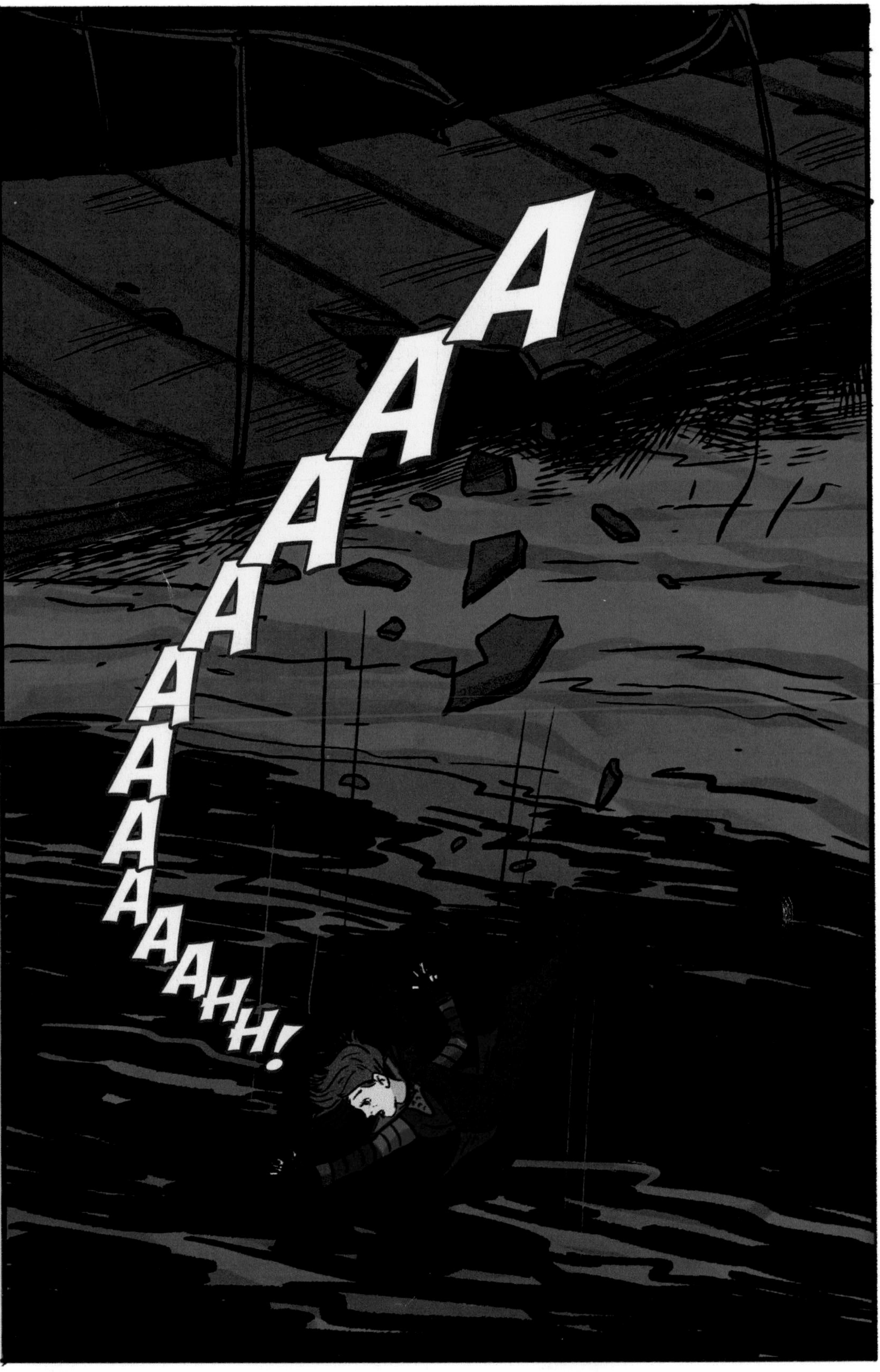
AAAAAAAAAAHH!

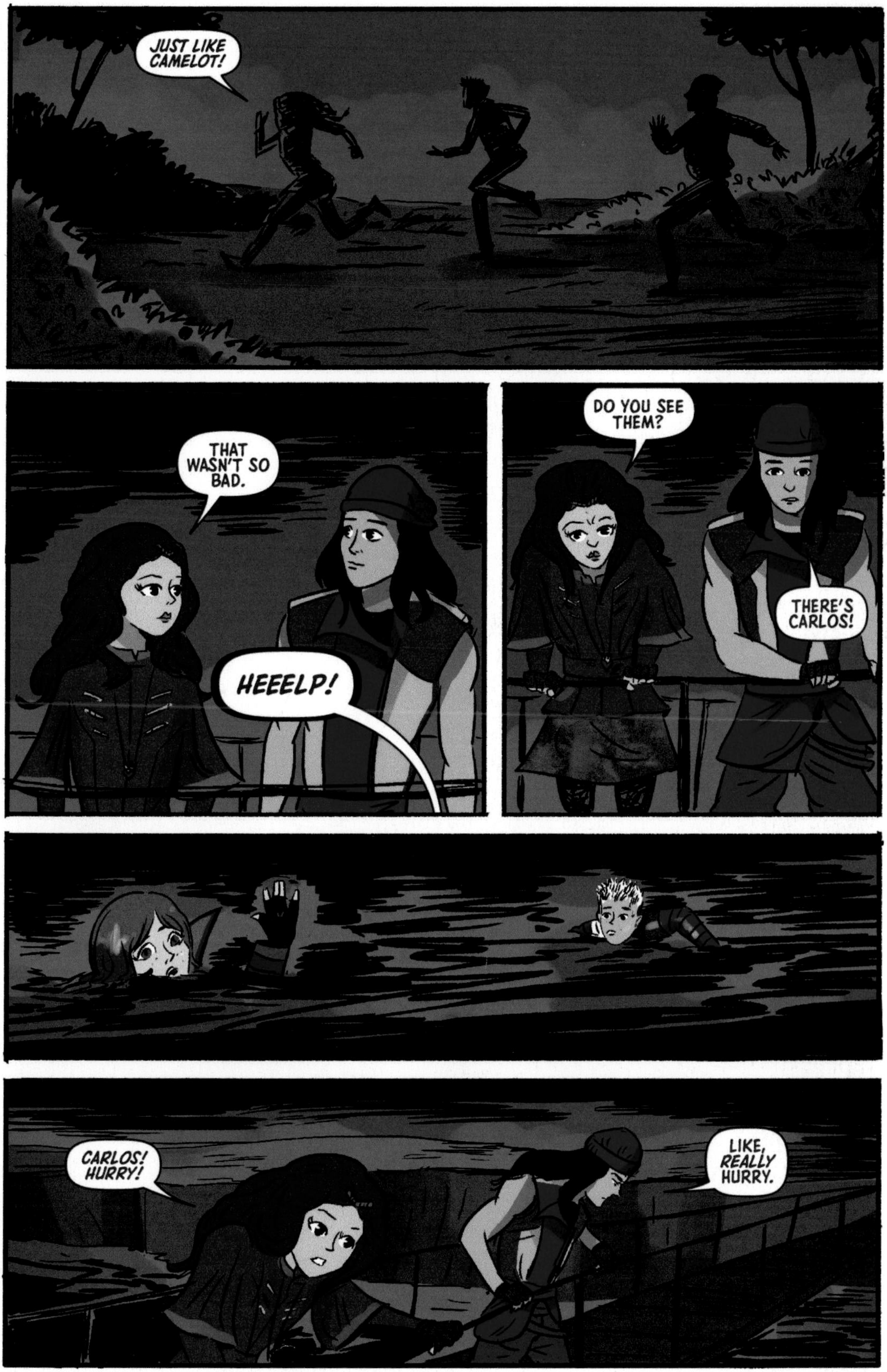
JUST LIKE CAMELOT!
THAT WASN'T SO BAD.
HEEELP!
DO YOU SEE THEM?
THERE'S CARLOS!
CARLOS! HURRY!
LIKE, REALLY HURRY.

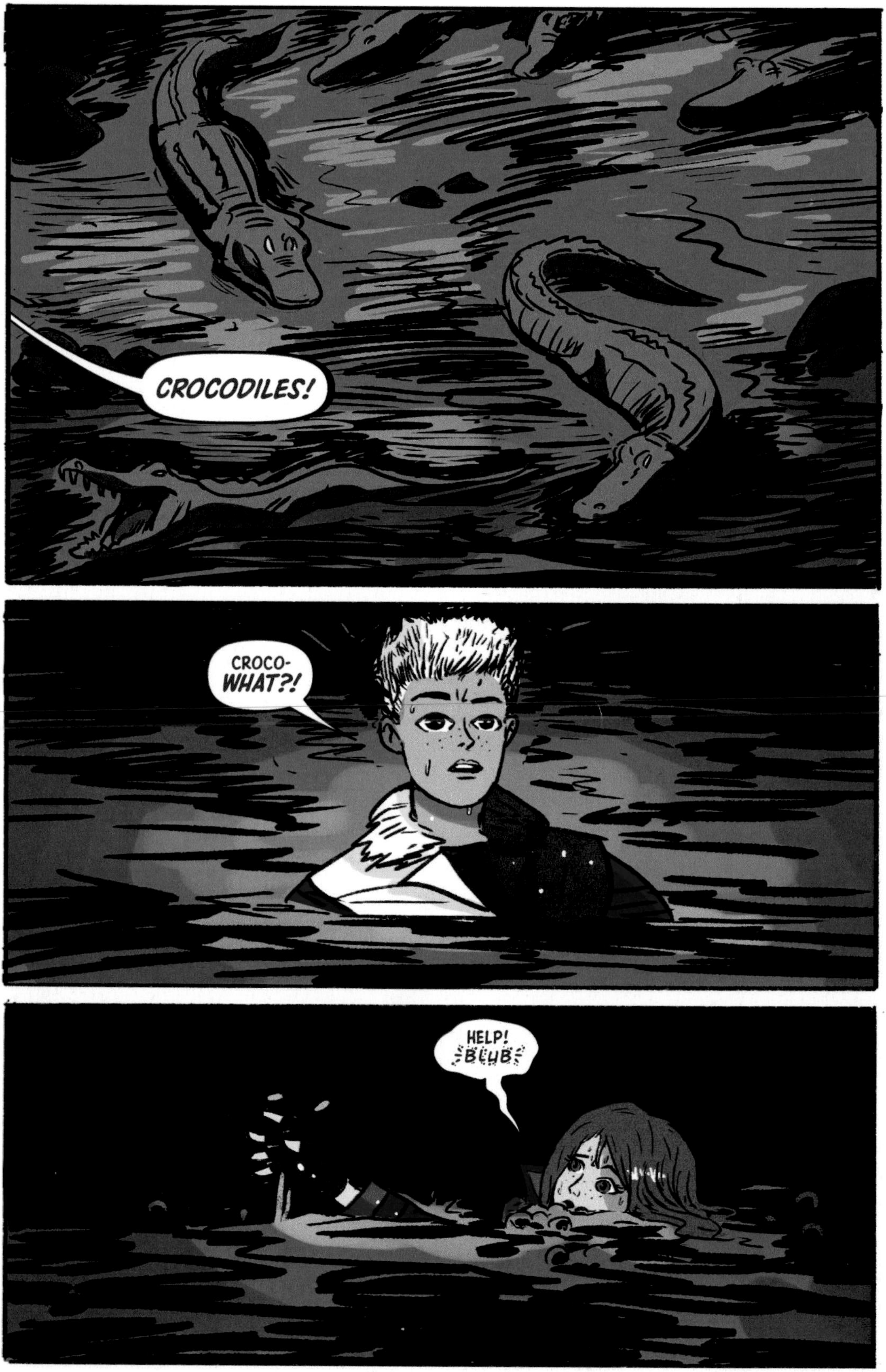
CROCODILES!
CROCO-
WHAT?!
HELP!
BLUB

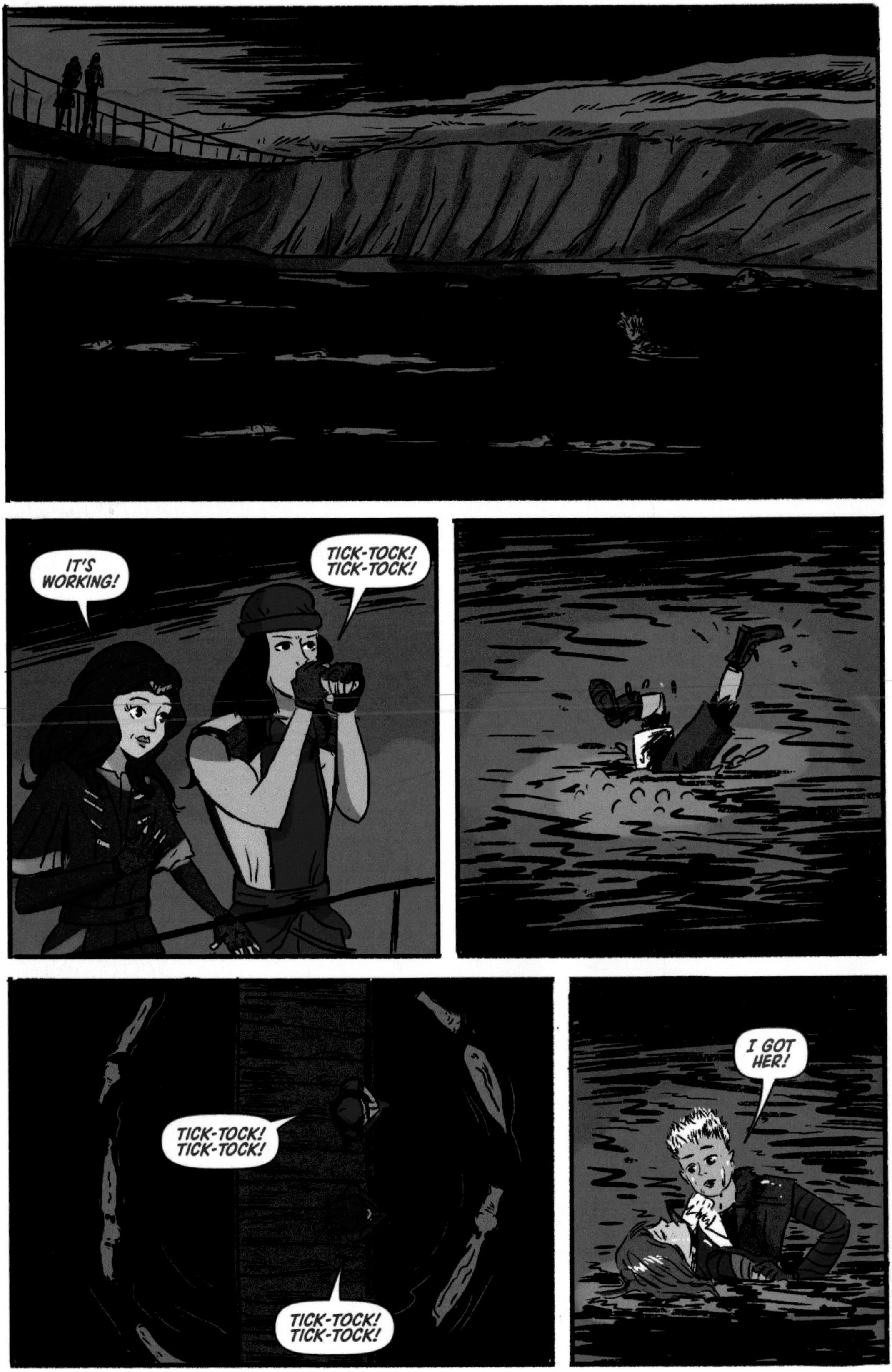
IT'S WORKING!
TICK-TOCK! TICK-TOCK!
TICK-TOCK! TICK-TOCK!
TICK-TOCK! TICK-TOCK!
I GOT HER!

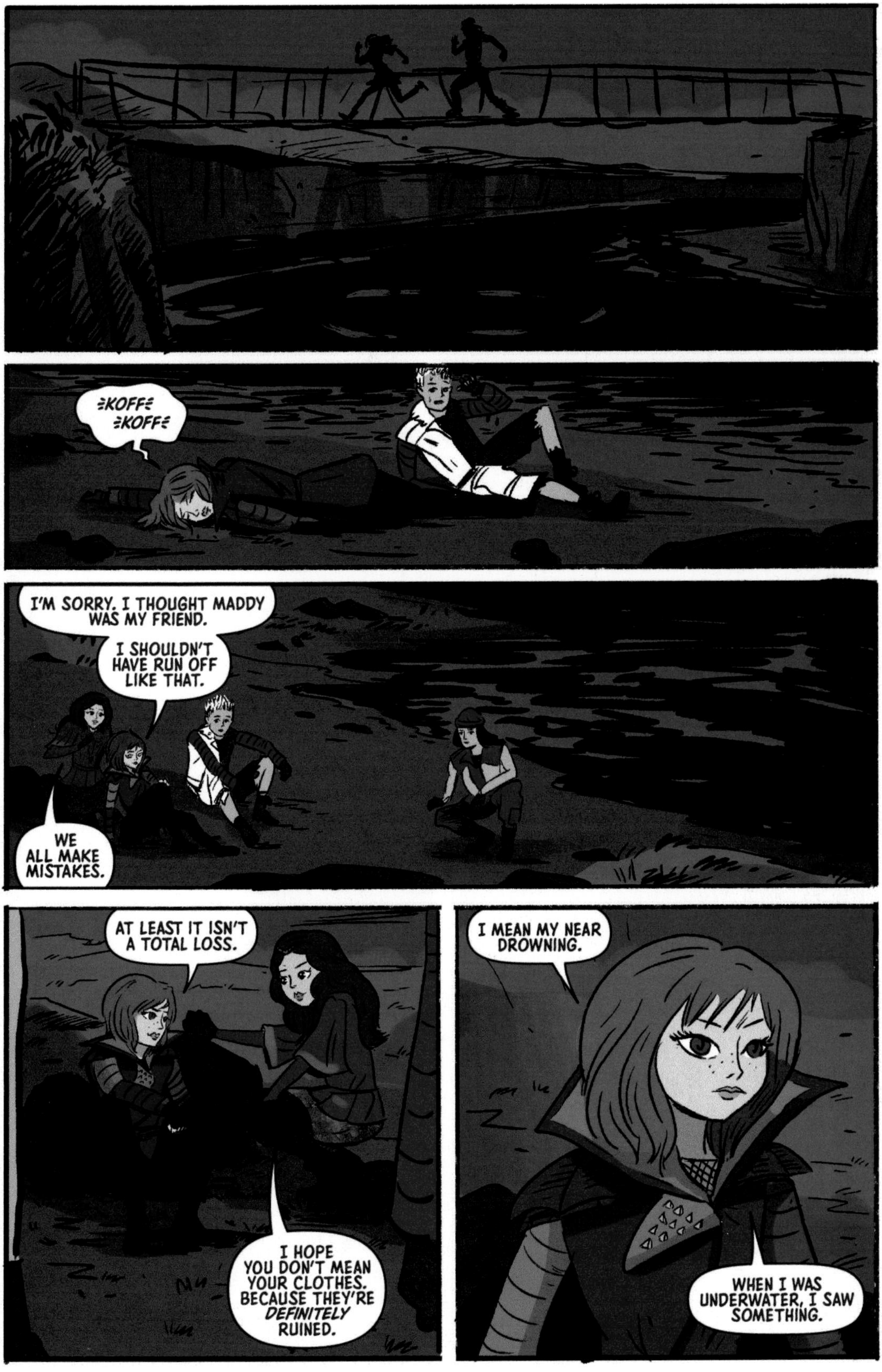
KOFF KOFF
I'M SORRY. I THOUGHT MADDY WAS MY FRIEND.
I SHOULDN'T HAVE RUN OFF LIKE THAT.
WE ALL MAKE MISTAKES.
AT LEAST IT ISN'T A TOTAL LOSS.
I HOPE YOU DON'T MEAN YOUR CLOTHES. BECAUSE THEY'RE *DEFINITELY* RUINED.
I MEAN MY NEAR DROWNING.
WHEN I WAS UNDERWATER, I SAW SOMETHING.

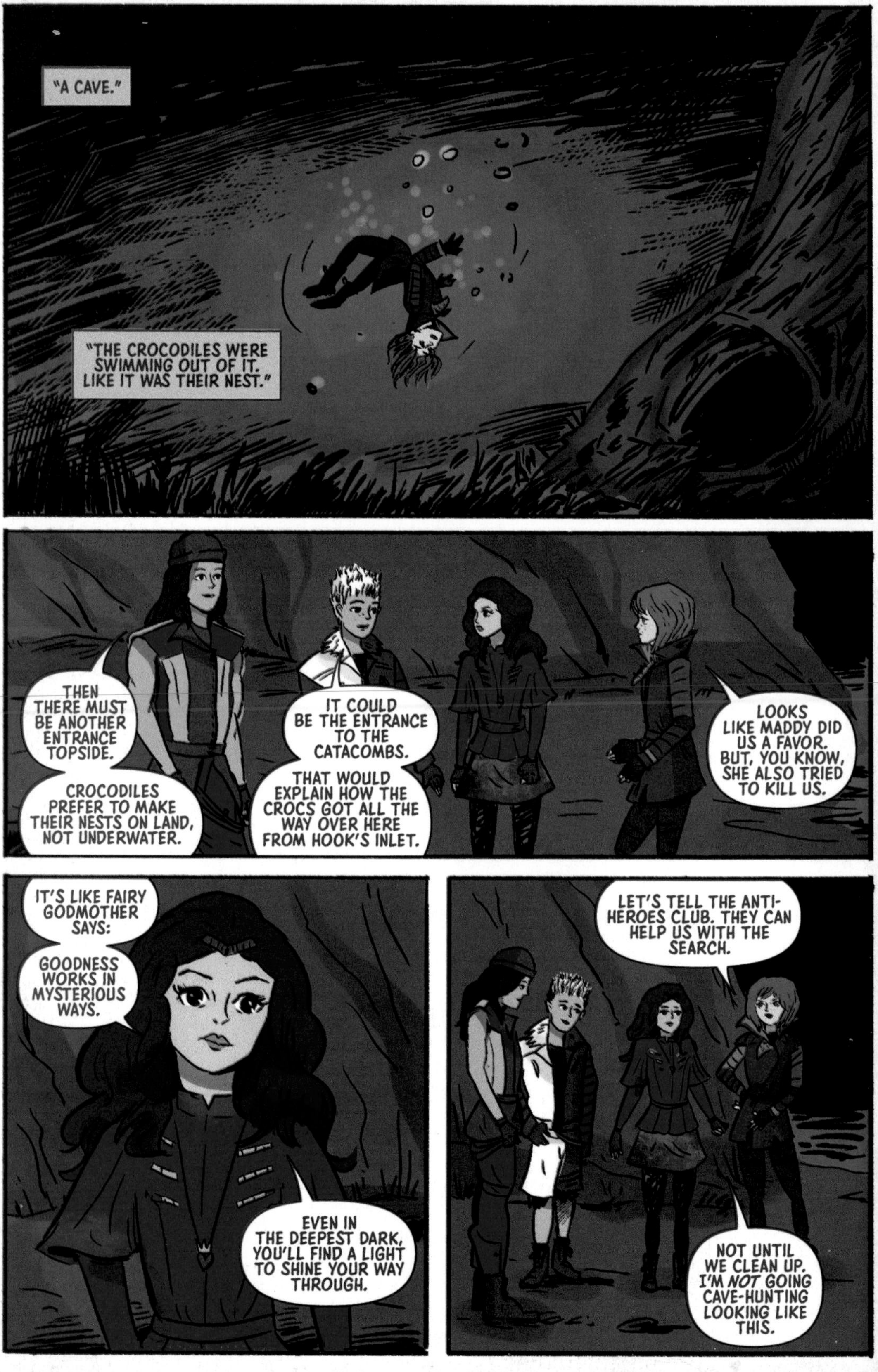
"A CAVE."
"THE CROCODILES WERE SWIMMING OUT OF IT. LIKE IT WAS THEIR NEST."
THEN THERE MUST BE ANOTHER ENTRANCE TOPSIDE.
CROCODILES PREFER TO MAKE THEIR NESTS ON LAND, NOT UNDERWATER.
IT COULD BE THE ENTRANCE TO THE CATACOMBS.
THAT WOULD EXPLAIN HOW THE CROCS GOT ALL THE WAY OVER HERE FROM HOOK'S INLET.
LOOKS LIKE MADDY DID US A FAVOR. BUT, YOU KNOW, SHE ALSO TRIED TO KILL US.
IT'S LIKE FAIRY GODMOTHER SAYS:
GOODNESS WORKS IN MYSTERIOUS WAYS.
EVEN IN THE DEEPEST DARK, YOU'LL FIND A LIGHT TO SHINE YOUR WAY THROUGH.
LET'S TELL THE ANTI-HEROES CLUB. THEY CAN HELP US WITH THE SEARCH.
NOT UNTIL WE CLEAN UP. I'M *NOT* GOING CAVE-HUNTING LOOKING LIKE THIS.

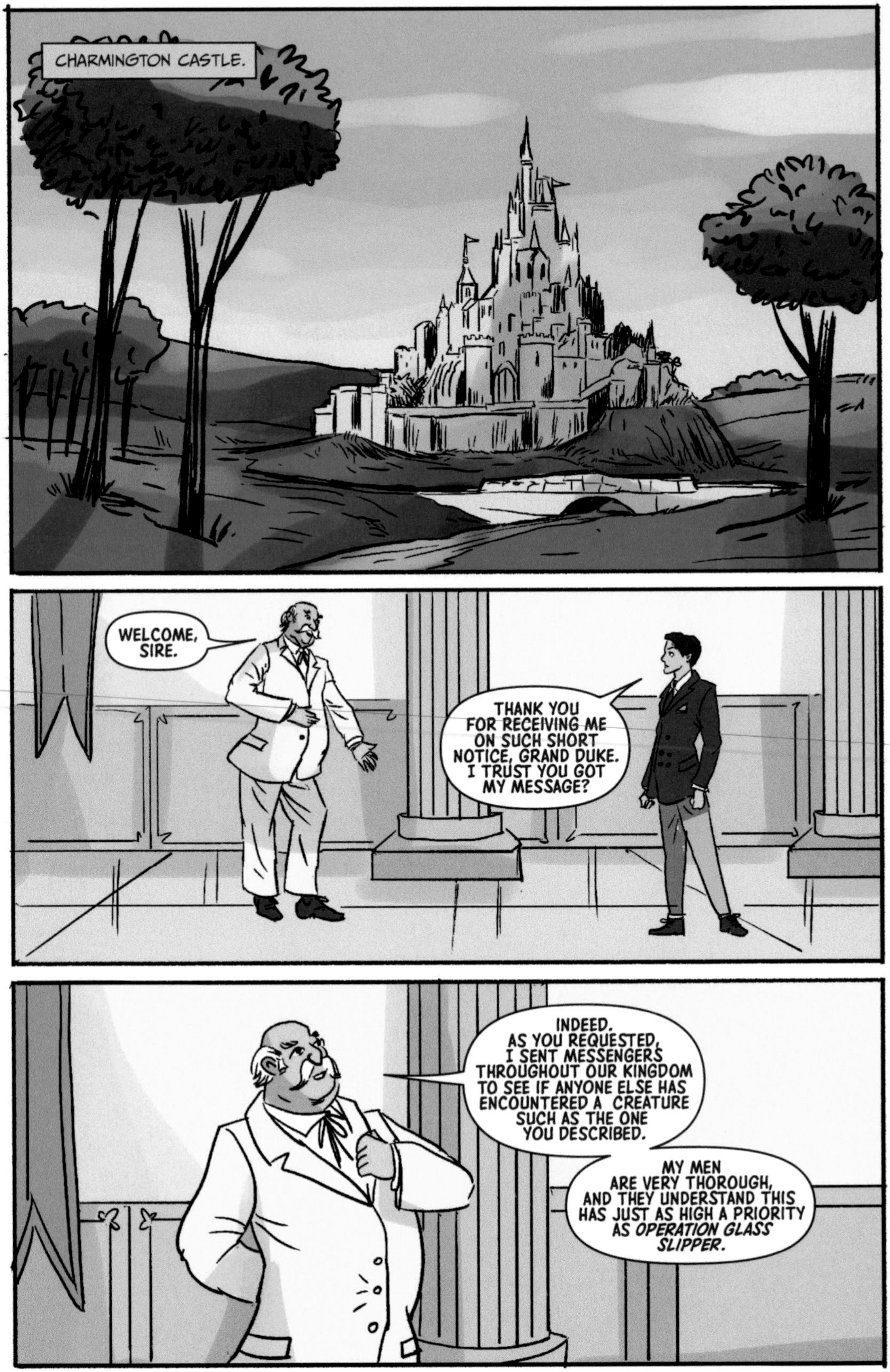
CHARMINGTON CASTLE.
WELCOME, SIRE.
THANK YOU FOR RECEIVING ME ON SUCH SHORT NOTICE, GRAND DUKE. I TRUST YOU GOT MY MESSAGE?
INDEED. AS YOU REQUESTED, I SENT MESSENGERS THROUGHOUT OUR KINGDOM TO SEE IF ANYONE ELSE HAS ENCOUNTERED A CREATURE SUCH AS THE ONE YOU DESCRIBED.
MY MEN ARE VERY THOROUGH, AND THEY UNDERSTAND THIS HAS JUST AS HIGH A PRIORITY AS *OPERATION GLASS SLIPPER*.

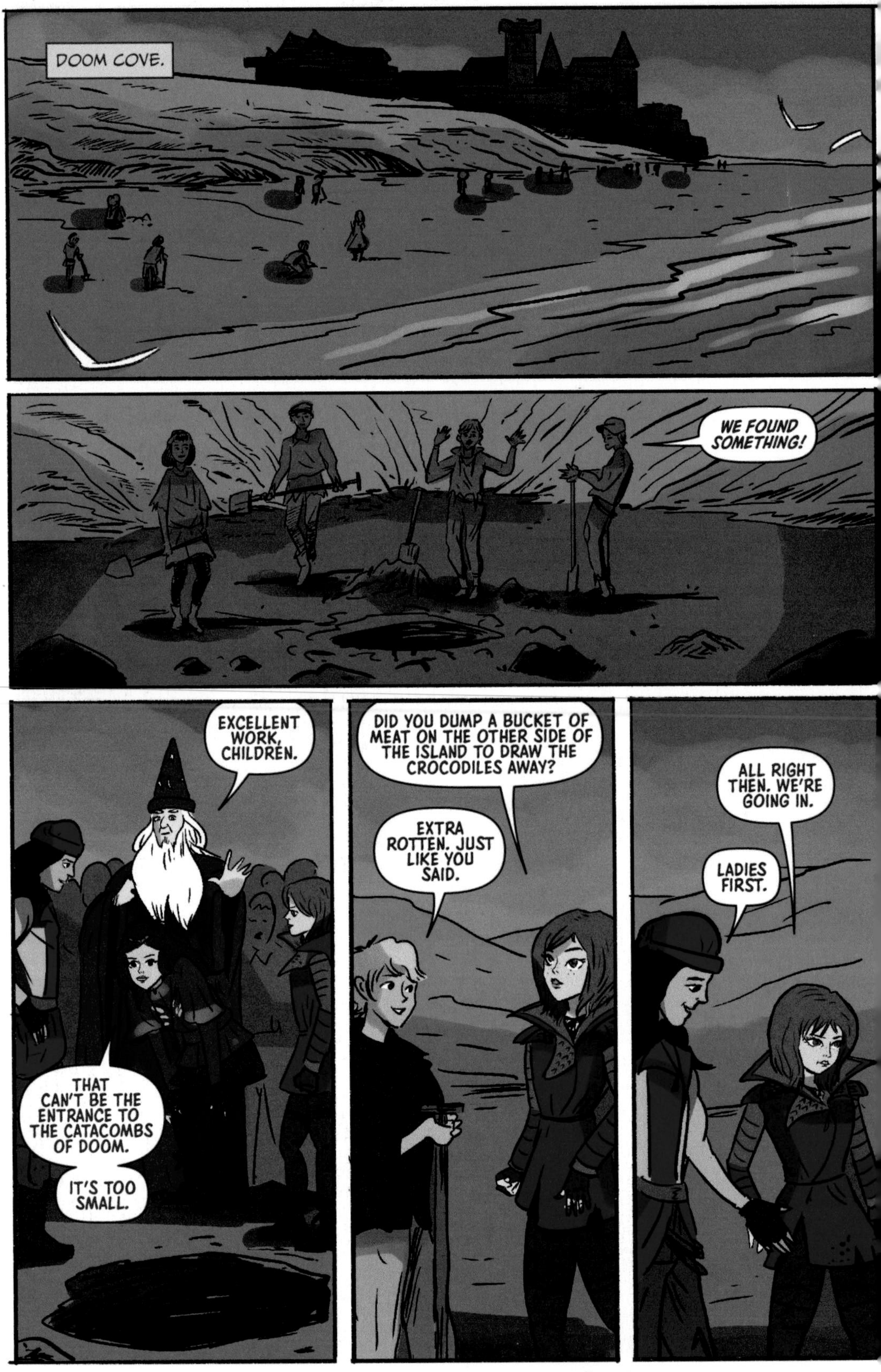
DOOM COVE.
WE FOUND SOMETHING!
EXCELLENT WORK, CHILDREN.
THAT CAN'T BE THE ENTRANCE TO THE CATACOMBS OF DOOM.
IT'S TOO SMALL.
DID YOU DUMP A BUCKET OF MEAT ON THE OTHER SIDE OF THE ISLAND TO DRAW THE CROCODILES AWAY?
EXTRA ROTTEN. JUST LIKE YOU SAID.
ALL RIGHT THEN. WE'RE GOING IN.
LADIES FIRST.

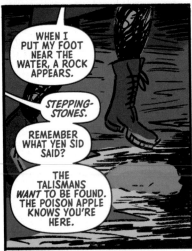

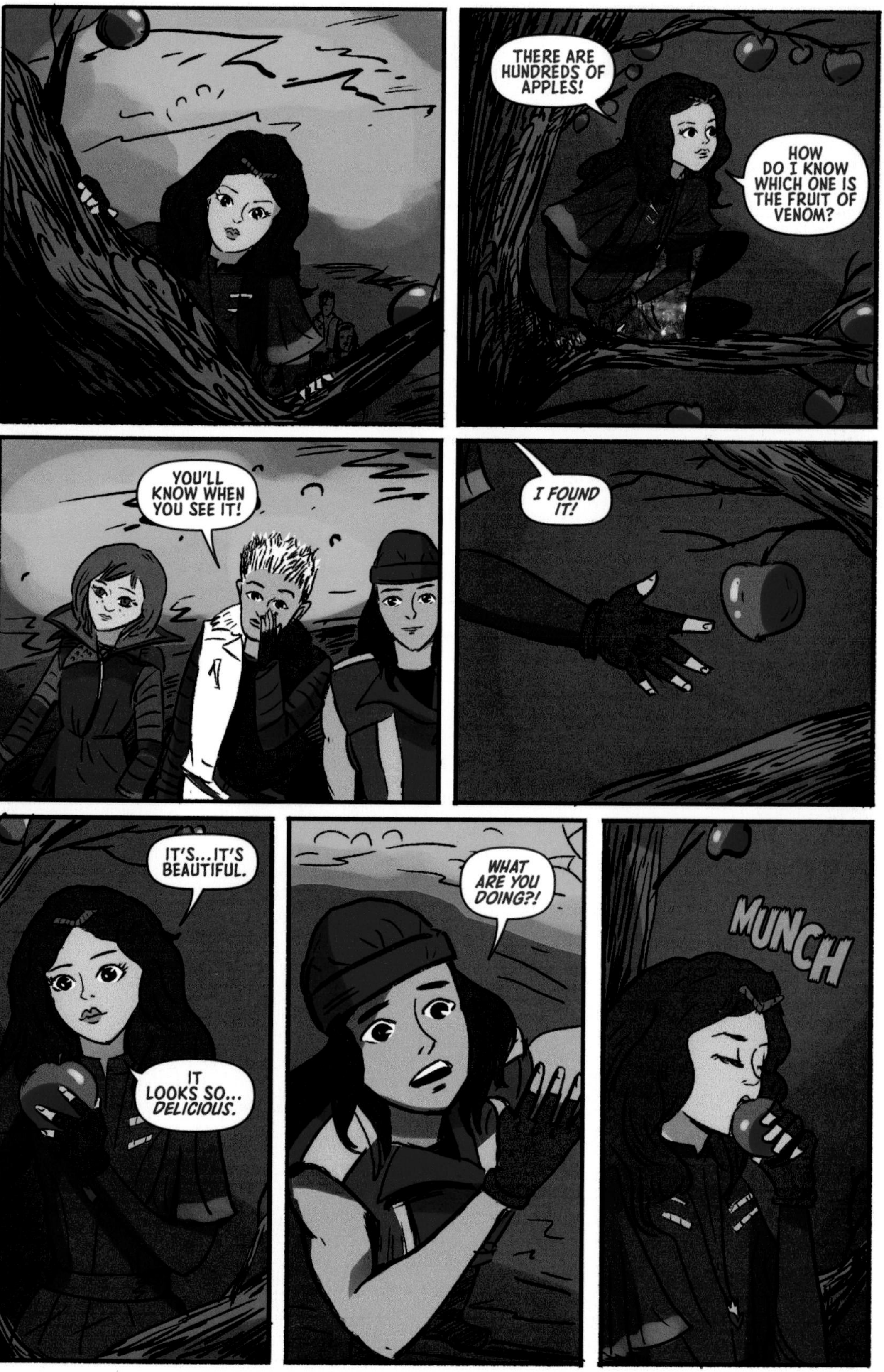
THERE ARE HUNDREDS OF APPLES!
HOW DO I KNOW WHICH ONE IS THE FRUIT OF VENOM?
YOU'LL KNOW WHEN YOU SEE IT!
I FOUND IT!
IT'S...IT'S BEAUTIFUL.
IT LOOKS SO... DELICIOUS.
WHAT ARE YOU DOING?!
MUNCH

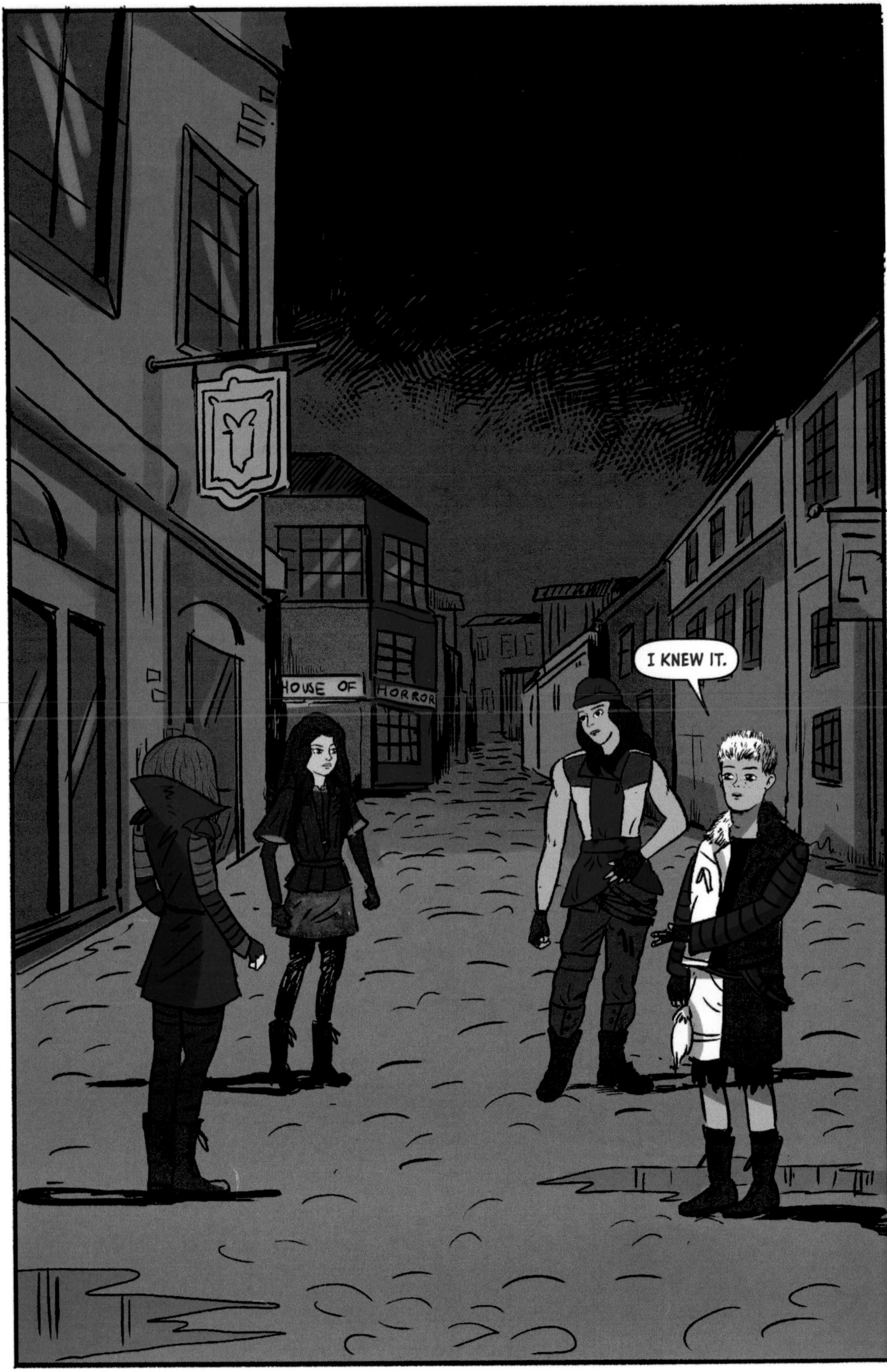
I KNEW IT.
HOUSE OF HORROR

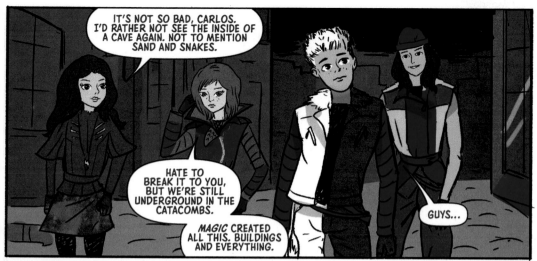

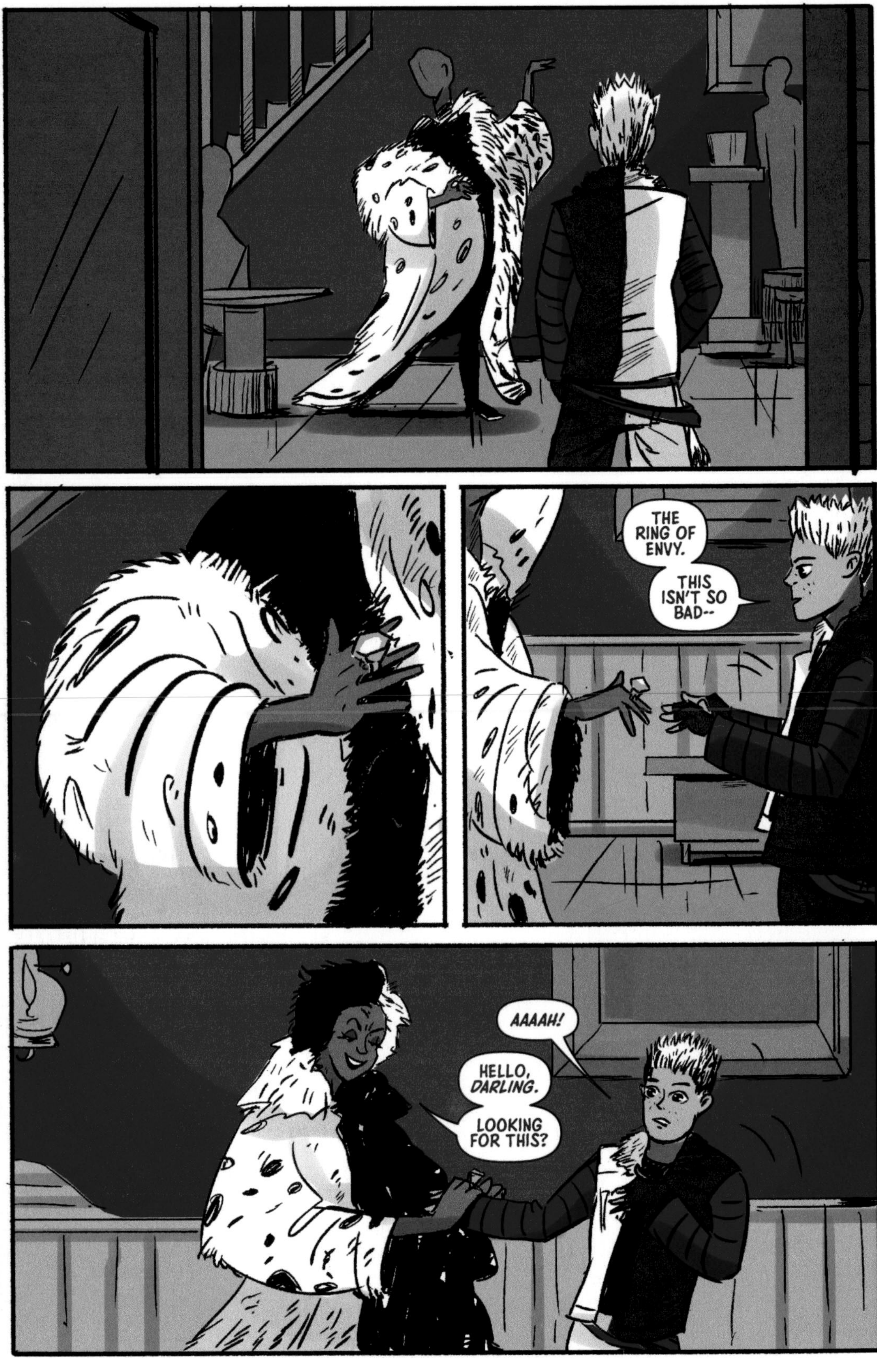
THE RING OF ENVY.
THIS ISN'T SO BAD--
AAAAH!
HELLO, *DARLING.*
LOOKING FOR THIS?

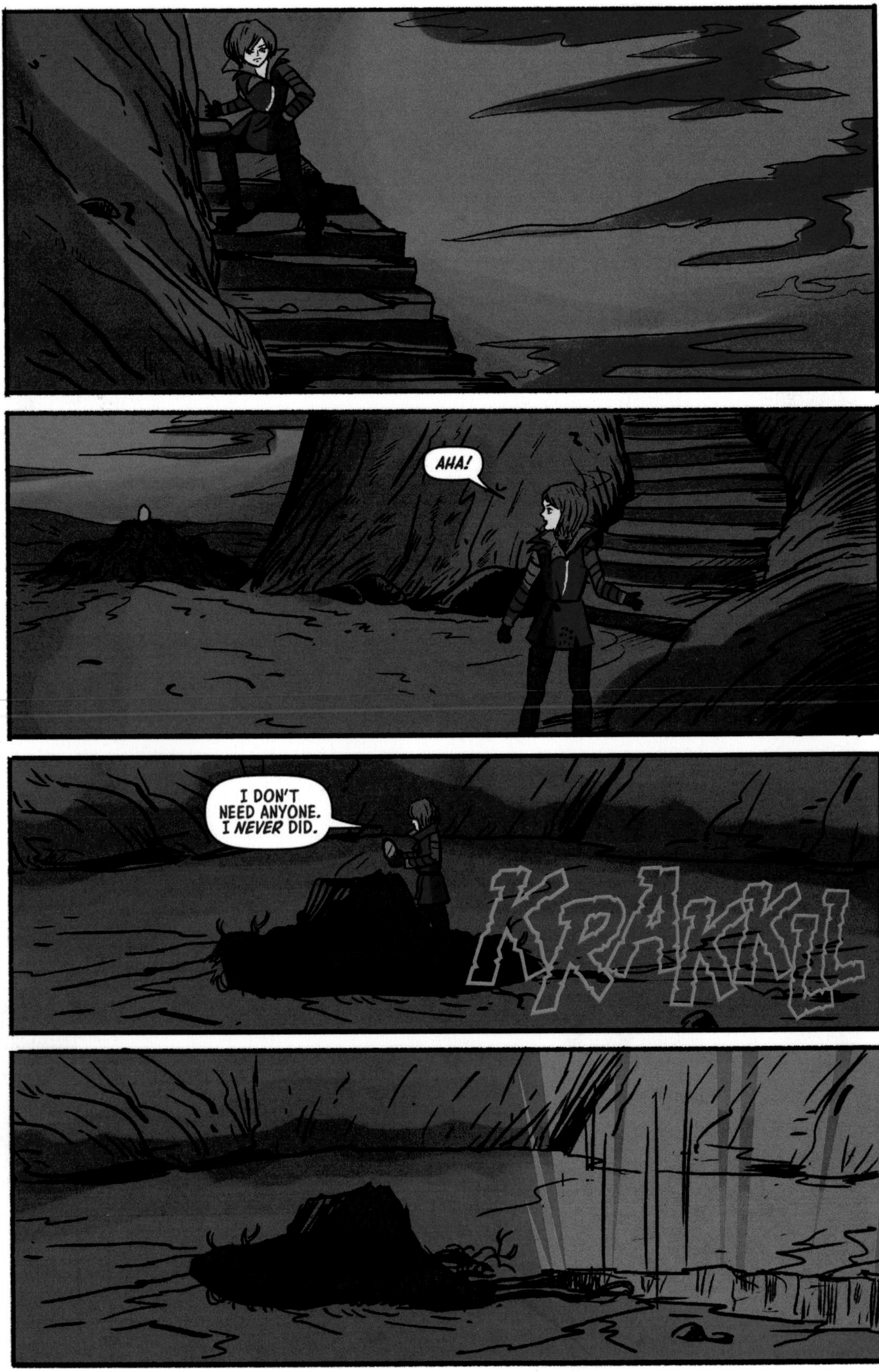
AHA!
I DON'T NEED ANYONE. I NEVER DID.
KRAKKL

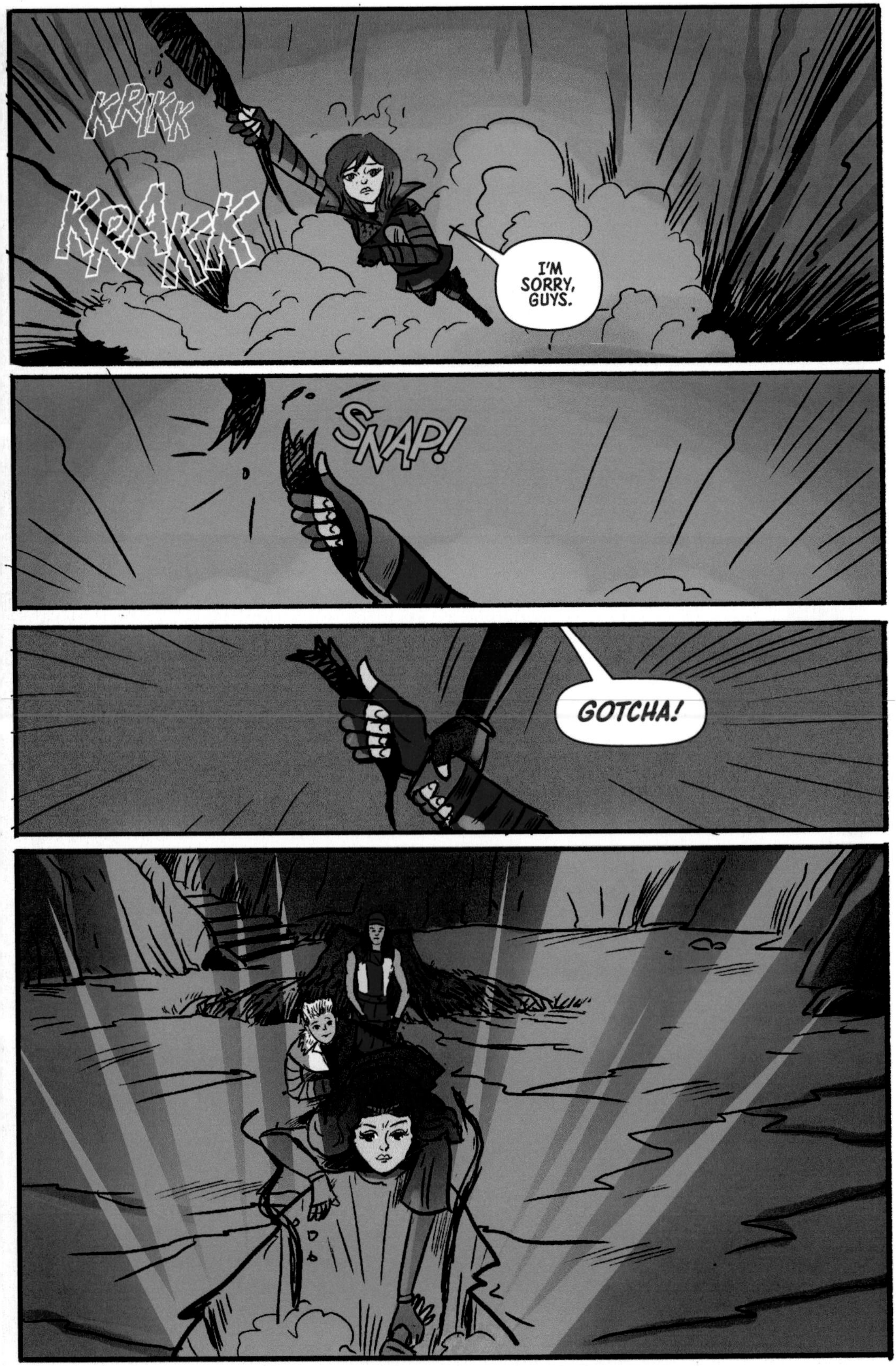
KRIKK
KRAKK
I'M SORRY, GUYS.
SNAP!
GOTCHA!

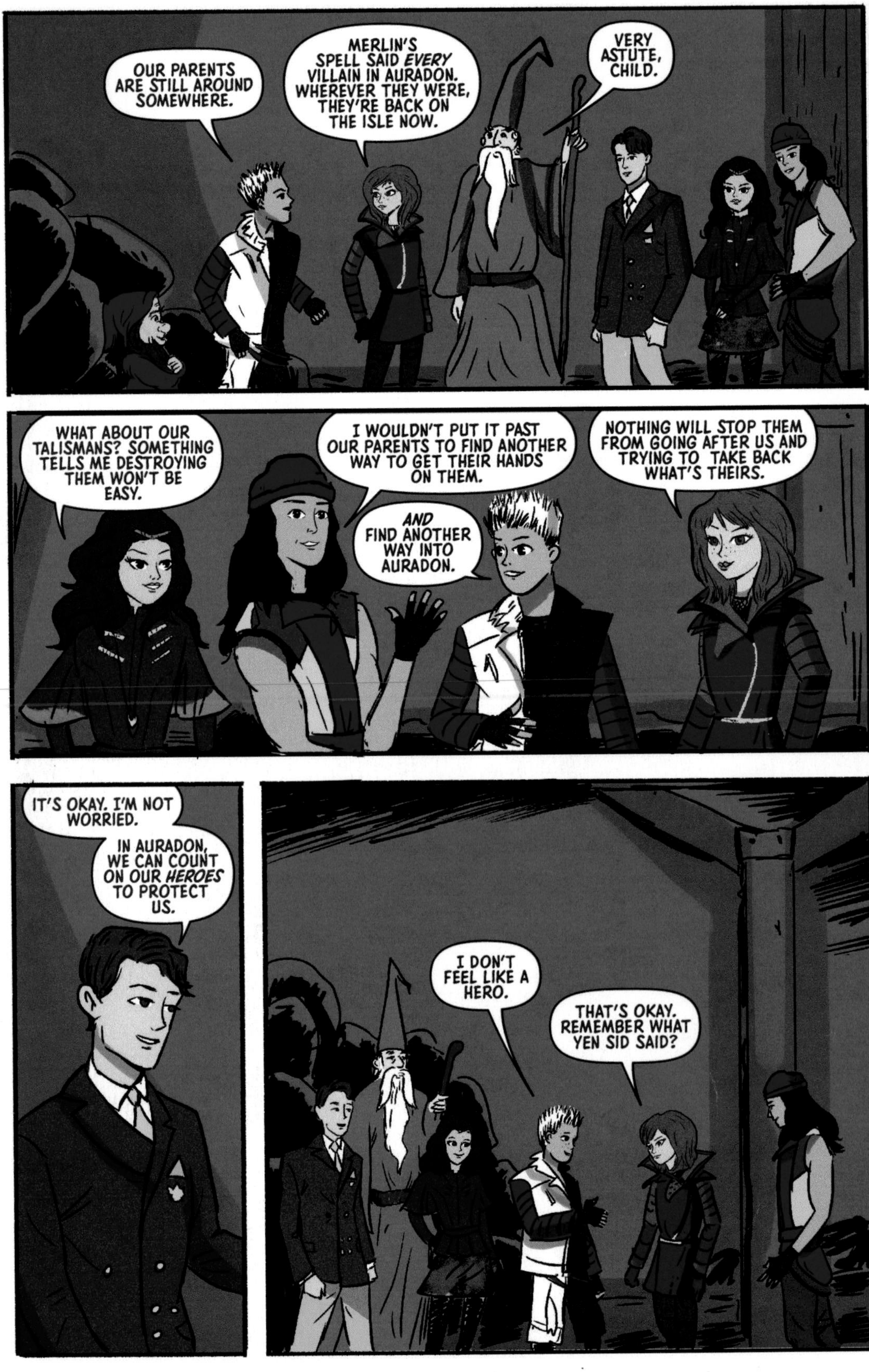
OUR PARENTS ARE STILL AROUND SOMEWHERE.
MERLIN'S SPELL SAID *EVERY* VILLAIN IN AURADON. WHEREVER THEY WERE, THEY'RE BACK ON THE ISLE NOW.
VERY ASTUTE, CHILD.
WHAT ABOUT OUR TALISMANS? SOMETHING TELLS ME DESTROYING THEM WON'T BE EASY.
I WOULDN'T PUT IT PAST OUR PARENTS TO FIND ANOTHER WAY TO GET THEIR HANDS ON THEM.
AND FIND ANOTHER WAY INTO AURADON.
NOTHING WILL STOP THEM FROM GOING AFTER US AND TRYING TO TAKE BACK WHAT'S THEIRS.
IT'S OKAY. I'M NOT WORRIED.
IN AURADON, WE CAN COUNT ON OUR *HEROES* TO PROTECT US.
I DON'T FEEL LIKE A HERO.
THAT'S OKAY. REMEMBER WHAT YEN SID SAID?

Sometimes being good
ISN'T SO BAD

THE #1 *NEW YORK TIMES* BEST SELLER BY
MELISSA DE LA CRUZ

the Isle of the Lost

A DESCENDANTS NOVEL

BOOK ONE

SEQUEL TO THE #1 *NEW YORK TIMES* BEST-SELLING *THE ISLE OF THE LOST*

Return to the Isle of the Lost

A DESCENDANTS NOVEL

BOOK TWO

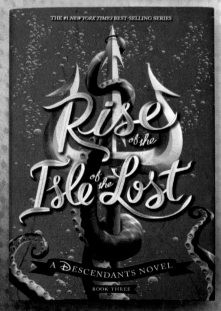

THE #1 *NEW YORK TIMES* BEST-SELLING SERIES

Rise of the Isle of the Lost

A DESCENDANTS NOVEL

BOOK THREE

BOOK THREE

THE #1 *NEW YORK TIMES* BEST-SELLING SERIES

Escape from the Isle of the Lost

A DESCENDANTS NOVEL

BOOK FOUR

BOOK FOUR

Disney·HYPERION   DISNEYDESCENDANTS.COM   DISNEYBOOKS.COM

WITHDRAWN